3

Priceless Jewel at the Well

The Diary of Rebekah's Nursemaid

Canaan

1986 B.C.–1985 B.C.

Diary One
Beersheba

1986 B.C.

In My Secret Place

I'm sheltered once again in my special, secret spot in the tamarisk grove. I love these trees with their willowy branches and slender leaves! Summer is here. The month of hostile heat is upon us, but my special trees don't care. They're covered with tiny pink-and-white clusters of flowers. Honeybees hover over the grove and won't let me near until later in the day. They abandon the grove then and fly away.

I've settled in a hollowed place in the dirt, which I fill with soft leaves and fallen petals. I also take care to pick out the hard twigs and dead debris that fall inside. My sister, Tova, discovered my secret place once when she followed me here. She noticed that I disappear each day when Mother no longer needs me to tend to Father. She said I've built a nest here, and she laughed. Lucky for me she lost interest and left me alone. I'm eleven, and Tova is two years older.

Yesterday I dug a hole deep enough to hide

you, little diary. Don't worry. I wrap you in a bit of goat-hair cloth so you stay good and clean. Then I push the mound of dirt back in place and cover you with branches and leaves. No one will ever find you here; and no one will ever be able to read my thoughts.

Father's eyesight began to fail after the raven appeared in our camp for the second time. That was a year ago, and he's almost blind now. He struggles to recognize the fuzzy shapes that pass in front of his frosted eyes. He calls the raven the creature of ill omen. He says it's the most prophetic of all birds, and it carries on its inky black wings the whisper of illness or death.

The raven first appeared five years ago. Father stood still in the camp, his head lifted toward the heavens. A tiny dark dot was painted in the sky. It grew larger and larger until I could hear the familiar swish of the raven's wings.

I watched the bird circle in a low arc and hang on a current of heated desert air. It seemed

6

suspended in midflight, and it taunted me to follow it, but Father grabbed my arm before I could
take a step. He held me close to him.

Then a gust of wind sent the bird soaring.
He croaked and spread his wings just beyond
our tents. He was so close that I could see the
tuft of black hair on his curved bill. Father's
eyes filled with sorrow, and he shook his head.
"We'll have bad news soon," he told Mother.
"It's not in our camp, but the bad news will
touch us. Prepare yourself."

I grabbed Mother's tunic and tugged on it
hard.

Her eyes were still fixed on the creature as it
flew into the glare of the sun.

"What does Father mean?" I asked her.
She bent down and took my hands in hers. "The
raven knows when ill fortune will be delivered
to a family, Alisah. Some say it can smell the
odor of decay from a long way away. It has
come today to warn us."

Two days later, a man sauntered into our
camp on a camel. His face was weathered with

age and sorrow, his head was shaved, and he wore dark, ill-fitting sackcloth. Another camel, without a rider, sashayed beside him. Father rose to his feet and waited for the traveler to approach.

"*Shalom alechem.* I am Eliezer, servant of Abraham," the man said. His words were deep and gravelly like the sound of grain when it's ground between a stone mortar and pestle.

"*Shalom alechem,*" Father replied. "I remember you well. I can see by your dress that someone dear to you has died. You have come to tell me about this death."

Tova and I peeked out of our tent. We were behind Father, so he couldn't see us.

Eliezer nodded. "It is my beloved master, Abraham. He will be buried in the field of Machpelah tomorrow."

The Field of Sorrow—Hebron

Father wasn't well enough to travel, so Mother and Tova and I began our journey north just hours after Eliezer brought us the news of

Abraham. I was six years old then. I shared a camel ride with Mother, and Tova shared one with Eliezer. Abraham was to be buried outside of Hebron deep within a limestone cave in hills ripe with fruit trees.

After many hours of travel, we waded through a valley of pale grains and green grasses and climbed the eastern slope to the field of Machpelah. It was long and wide. Rocks marked off the field's boundaries. Mother said Abraham had purchased this field and cave forty-eight years earlier to bury his beloved wife, Sarah.

I stood on a grassy knoll that day between my sister and my mother. The wind whipped through the open cave, then moaned with sorrow as it blew out and passed through the veils, tunics, and sackcloths of the gathered mourners. The sky, usually a deep, clear blue, was the color of a sun-weathered stone. There were cries of grief and the lonely, haunting wail of the pipe.

My mother clutched my hand and pulled me close to her. She didn't look at me while she adjusted my veil with her small fingers. We wore identical black cloths over our heads and the lower half of our faces. I remember how my hair stuck to my head and how my own breath threatened to suffocate me beneath that mourning veil. I reached up and lowered it and tasted the fresh air with my tongue. Mother lifted it back up without a word of reproach.

She bent close to my ear. "Alisah, the two men nearest the cave are Isaac and Ishmael. They are Abraham's sons."

Ishmael was a head taller than Isaac, and his skin was dark in comparison. The sackcloth was stretched taut over his back, and I could see that his arms and shoulders were muscular and broad. A quiver was slung over his shoulder. Mother told me later that his mother, Hagar, was an Egyptian. I realize now that this would account for Ishmael's unusual height. His quiver told me, even then, that he was an archer. This would account for his broad shoulders.

Their bare heads, shaven in grief, were sprinkled with dust and ash to show their sorrow. Isaac also wore the coarse sackcloth upon his back.

Then Mother inclined her head toward a beautiful woman. Her eyes were downcast, and her long black hair, woven in a simple braid, was hung over her slender shoulder. "That's Rebekah, Isaac's wife. Their twin sons, Jacob and Esau, stand beside her. They must be fifteen years old by now."

I couldn't pull my eyes from Rebekah. She was beautiful like Tova, with her creamy skin and blue-black hair. My sister stood beside me that day with tears in her enormous dark eyes. She was eight at the time, and even though she had seen Abraham but once or twice in her life, she felt the loss of a great man. Tova is sensitive like that.

My attention was drawn to the woman beside Rebekah. Her stooped back was turned to me. Two gray braids hung like thick ropes down to the small of her bent back. She turned suddenly, and her glittering black eyes bore through me. I was sure she could read my thoughts, and I slid behind Mother's legs. I hid my face until I saw that she had turned away.

"Who is that?" I asked Mother and pointed. Mother wrapped my finger in her hand and frowned at me. "That must be Deborah, Rebekah's nurse. It's been a long time since I last laid my eyes on her."

I'd never seen any of these people before that day. Our only connection to them was through Rhoda, who had been Sarah's traveling companion long, long ago. Stories about Rhoda and Sarah and Abraham had been passed down through our family for years. Though Sarah died long before I was born, she was mother to us all, just as Abraham was our father.

My father had taken my sister and me to visit Abraham once when I was just old enough to walk. He was a beautiful, ancient man with long, silken white hair. His beard flowed from his chin like goats' milk from a skin. His smile was as kind as his eyes were wise.

I think of Abraham often when I sit in my special spot here among the tamarisks. His presence is everywhere. There's an old well beside the trees. Father said it was dug by Abraham. He said Abraham made a covenant with God when he dug the well, and then he planted the first tamarisk tree of the grove. Maybe that's why I love this spot so much. It must be a holy place. I know I feel peaceful and serene when I'm here.

When Abraham died, the Philistines thundered across the plain to Beersheba and stopped up all seven of Abraham's wells. They filled them with rock and dirt. Father dug another well then, closer to our camp. He built a wall of stones around the hole so we wouldn't fall into it.

Whenever I need to think and my head is clouded with thoughts, I come here between the trees and watch the graceful branches stir around me. I've even fallen asleep here with my head resting on a small mat. I'm often awakened by the flutter of a dove's wings just above me or the tickle of a harmless lizard as it scurries over my foot.

Oh my. I just heard my mother's voice. "Aleeeeesaaaah!" She trills like a songbird when she calls to me. I must go.

Much Later

The palms of my hands are fluttering beneath the skin. It always happens to me when I feel uneasy. An air of foreboding hangs in the camp like a storm cloud. I returned from my secret place earlier when Mother called to me, and I could tell that Father was disturbed. He paced in the dirt in front of his tent, ten paces in either direction until his feet had worn a neat path.

Mother had already begun the preparations for supper, and Tova was busy beside her. It would be another light meal. Since Father is unable to tend the flocks now, many of them have disappeared, one by one, into the night. Five goats and ten sheep are all that remain. Tova has taken it upon herself to watch them as best she can, but Mother won't allow her to stay with them when darkness falls.

"It's no place for a young woman," she said, and Father agreed. "There are wild animals and thieves. How can a girl like Tova fight them off?

She has no meat on her bones as it is."

Tova has plenty of meat on her bones that I can see, but never enough to please Mother. She pinches our cheeks and our arms and anywhere she can reach. If a mound of our flesh doesn't fit between her thumb and her pointer finger, she wails in anguish.

"How will I be able to marry you two off if you don't eat? Do you think any decent young man wants to marry a sack of bones? What pleasure will he find in a sack of bones?"

Father used to laugh at this, but not anymore. He carries the burden of guilt because there isn't enough food to go around.

I grabbed the milk jug and walked to the goats beyond our camp. I heard Tova shuffle a few steps behind me.

"I tried to milk them at daybreak," she called to me. "They're just too thin now. You won't get much."

She was right. I did manage to coax a few squirts of milk into the jug, but I stared at it in disbelief. It wasn't rich and creamy anymore, but thin and watery. I sat on the ground. For the first time in a long time, I wanted to cry. I'm too big to cry, but two fat tears welled up in my eyes, and Tova saw them. She sat beside me and put her arm around me.

"Alisah, I want to talk to you." Tova's eyebrows were knit together, and she licked her lips. "We have to help Mother and Father. We have no brothers to help Father tend the flocks, and he grows worse each day. Our situation grows worse. Soon there will be no food to eat."

"I know," I told her in earnest, "but I don't know what we can do. Father won't let you graze the flocks farther away, and I can't . . ."

She interrupted me with a wave of her hand. "Hush, little sister. I have a plan if you'll allow me to speak."

I was silent and she continued.

"I'll marry Guni. His family can pay Father a good price for me, and he and I can continue to live with Mother and Father for as long as necessary. Guni is an excellent shepherd, and he can grow crops here. The soil is good. Father likes him very much."

I stared at Tova. She spoke of her marriage like it was a business arrangement between two neighbors. We've known Guni for years. Tova regards him as a friend, but I never thought she'd marry him.

I picked up a small stick and doodled in the yellow-brown soil. I knew she wasn't finished yet, so I waited for her to gather her thoughts. Afterward, I'd express my opinion. I always do.

"There's something else." Tova squeezed my shoulders. "Do you remember Abraham's funeral?"

"Of course." I wondered what this had to do with anything.

"Do you remember Rebekah and her nurse Deborah?"

I nodded.

"Well, I overheard Mother and Father," Tova continued. "It seems Deborah is ninety years old, and she isn't able to keep up with her duties as well as she used to. Rebekah has advised her to bring in a young girl to help in the household."

I felt uneasy. I didn't like the tone of Tova's voice. She spoke with too much caution, and she studied my face intently.

"Yes, so what does this have to do with us?" I couldn't mask the irritation in my voice.

"Well, Rebekah won't hear of a stranger coming into her house," Tova replied.

"And . . . ," I coaxed her.

"Our family is well respected," she explained. "We aren't direct kin, but we have distant ties with Abraham and Sarah through Rhoda. Deborah remembers you from the funeral. You're the perfect age, and they've already extended an invitation for you to join them in their household."

I was stunned. I felt betrayed by my own sister. Tova must have seen the hurt in my eyes, because she pulled me closer to her. "I don't want you to go away." Her voice was hoarse, and I thought now that *she* would cry. "Just like I don't know if I really want to marry Guni."

"Then why do we have to do this? Why can't we just tell everyone no? There must be another way." I heard my voice rise, and I knew I sounded like a selfish child, but I didn't care.

"Because we're young women now, and we have to help Mother and Father," Tova replied. "I'll marry Guni, and then they'll have a son to care for them. One day you'll marry too, and they'll have another son."

I didn't want to disagree with her, but I didn't tell her that I agreed either.

"Be brave," she whispered, "just as I will be. Isaac is very generous, and he loves and serves Yahweh. Father says he is a *tamin,* a good and gentle soul, and so is Rebekah. They'll pay you wages, and you can use your wages to help care for Mother and Father. We must all work together now."

Mother called to us. I could hear by her voice that she was annoyed. She had been waiting all this time for the goats' milk. I looked into the jug and held it sideways. The two lean squirts of milk had run together to form a large teardrop on the bottom.

The Next Day

We're about to receive a visitor, so I don't have long to finish my story. Last evening, after Tova and I returned to camp, our family shared a quiet, sad supper of bread, figs, and olives. We all sensed that great change was just a breath away.

I'm afraid. I've never lived away from my home before, and I have no desire to start now. Mother told me before I fell asleep last night that someone from Isaac's household would be here for me in two days.

I can't reveal my true feelings to Mother. Tova and I agreed that we should act as normal as possible. This will make it easier for her.

"I don't know when you'll be allowed to visit," said Mother in a small voice, "but I'm sure we can work it out." She combed my hair and smoothed it with her hands.

I put my hand over hers and squeezed it twice. This is our secret code. It means, "I love you." She squeezed mine twice in return.

"I'm sure they'll allow me to visit my own Mother and Father," I reassured her and even tried to laugh a little. "Tova tells me they're very good people, and they love and serve Yahweh."

"Yes, yes, that's right," Mother agreed. Her eyes were vacant as she spoke. I could tell she was far away from me. She was already lost in thoughts of the days ahead.

Tova was on her bed mat. A wick, suspended in a puddle of olive oil, burned in a clay lamp beside her. She had listened in silence until now. "Father says Guni will pay us a visit tomorrow," she said softly.

"Yes, yes," Mother replied. Half of her face was lit, and the other was in shadows. A small smile touched the corners of her mouth. "He's a good man, that Guni. His father, Zaccai, son of Iram, is known for his skill as a shepherd and provider. It's an honor to our family that they have chosen our Tova to marry their son."

I peered with caution at my sister. Her head was lowered so Mother couldn't see her eyes. She had loosened her hair from her braid, and her black locks were draped over her shoulders like a mourning veil.

"I think it's a good thing for Guni and his father that they've picked someone as beautiful and good as Tova," I said.

Tova looked up at me and smiled.

She has a beautiful smile, my sister, and I have a pang deep inside of me at the thought of leaving her. I must help Mother and Father ready our camp to receive my future brother-in-law. It's nearly noon, and he's sure to arrive soon. I promise, friend, to write in a short while and tell you all the news.

We Had a Visitor

At last Guni and his father have left. They don't live far away, so they'll have time to reach their camp before sunset. I've slipped away into the trees for a short while. I won't be missed. Mother and Father are talking in earnest with Tova.

I'm bathed in waves of sadness again and

again. My sister is betrothed. This should be one of the happiest days of her life, but it's filled with many emotions for all of us. Guni arrived with his father not long after I last wrote to you. Mother saw them from several acres away. Father heard the rhythmic clomp of the donkey's hooves long before they were visible to any of us.

I watched him incline his ear and knit his brows together. "Do you see them now, Mother?" he asked her again.

"Yes, yes, Silas, I told you I see them."

"Then, tell me, Mother, how many sheep are with them?"

I wasn't surprised. Since Father lost his sight, his hearing has been acute. He hears what the rest of us can't. He knew there were sheep trailing the two men before any of us saw their shadows on the horizon. It's a game he plays often to tease us, but he takes great delight in it.

Mother opened her mouth and then shut it again when Father held up his hand. "Wait!" he cried." I know! There are six—no wait, ten, yes, ten—sheep," he exclaimed.

Tova and I laughed and waited.

"That's not all!" he continued. "Goats! At least ten of those as well." He turned his head toward us. "Is that right, my girls? Count them. Tell me if your father is right again!"

I stood on my toes and tried to count them. They were still far enough away that I had to strain my eyes. Yes! It looked like there were ten of each!

"Yes, Father! You're right again!" I giggled.

Mother was tense now. "Girls, busy yourselves. Tova, you can fetch the water. We don't want to give the impression that we are idle." She disappeared into her tent, and I heard her shuffle about. Tova gathered two empty jugs and carried them to our well on the far side of camp.

I used this moment to have a word with Father. I reached out and placed my hand over his. "Why does he come with so many animals?" I asked.

"He's prepared to make an offer for your sister today," he said. "It's his *mohar*."

"What's a *mohar*?"

Father looked serious. "It's the bride-price. If a man wishes to marry a young woman, he must compensate her father for her value and for his loss. Do you know what the going price for a daughter is these days, my littlest one?"

I didn't like this question. What is the value of a daughter? How could one measure the value of a daughter, or anyone for that matter?

Father's head sank toward my face. "I know what you must think. I know because I've thought it too. There's nothing Guni can offer me that would equal the value of my daughter. They say I should accept no less than fifty shekels or the equivalent in animals or goods. What do you say?"

I was quiet and thought about this for a good while before I answered. "I say you should accept no less than what they tell you, Father, but Guni should pay a bit extra. I'll be losing a sister as well. I'll miss her very much."

My Sister Is Betrothed

Guni and Zaccai walked in the direction of our well. Zaccai stopped and waited while his son got off his donkey and approached Tova. She offered him a drink from the jug, and he tilted his head back and drank for a long time. She brought the jug to his father, and then the two men led the flocks to our pen. Tova followed behind as they walked toward our tents.

Father stood up to welcome them into the camp, and Mother rushed out with bowls of water so they could wash the travel dust from their feet. My sister and I prepared hot bread with a bit of barley flour, and I stirred the pot of porridge we'd cooked earlier. It was thick with wheat, barley, millet, and beans, and I added a bit more olive oil and camels' milk to thin it. It was a common man's stew, but it was all we had. Or so I thought.

Mother, as it turned out, surprised us all. She reached into a sack and pulled out a handful of meaty, brown walnuts. Then her hand dipped into another sack and produced ripe figs. From another sack she pulled olives softened in brine. My sister gasped. "Mother! You've hidden food all this time!"

She gave Tova a cross look. "Your mother has no need to hide anything. I saved this food for this very occasion. Would you have preferred to offer your future husband common locusts?"

Tova smiled and wrapped her arms around Mother. She whispered her thanks in her ear. *"Toda raba, toda raba."*

"All right then," Mother told her and thrust the bowls of food into her hands. "Now serve our guests a good meal."

Tova served the food, and Father offered the traditional blessing. "Blessed are you, Adonai our God, ruler of the universe, who brings forth bread from the earth." Then Guni and his father feasted.

When they'd finished, Guni held out two gold coins toward Tova. Father jabbed Tova in the ribs and signaled for her to take them.

I walked to Mother and put my arms around her soft middle. "That was the *kinyan*," she said in a hushed voice. "The groom must give the bride a gift of small value. Now watch. Guni will present our Tova with *mattan*."

She saw my puzzled expression. "They're love gifts. The two will be betrothed for a long time. These gifts from Guni will help Tova remember him and think warm thoughts of him until he returns for her on their wedding day."

She was right. Guni reached into the pocket of his girdle and pulled out a small leather pouch. When Tova reached inside, I heard a cry of glee escape from her lips. I inched closer, but Mother grasped the cloth of my tunic and pulled me back.

Tova had heard. She turned around and extended her arm so Mother and I could see. In the palm of her callused hand was a golden hairpin. Tiny red jewels were encrusted along the length it. Beside it was an ivory hair comb.

Mother put her hand over her mouth, and I could see Zaccai and Guni smile with pleasure.

Tova couldn't stop fingering the beautiful hair jewelry.

After a time, Tova's suitor cleared his throat and pulled a roll of papyrus from the fold of his leather girdle.

"What is it now?" I asked Mother.

"It must be the *ketubah,*" she replied. "It's the marriage contract. Guni is required to write down the amount of the *mohar,* the rights of the bride, and the promises of the groom. Father must agree to all of these things."

"But Father can't read now!" I cried.

"Shh!" she silenced me. "Watch Guni."

I watched him unroll the papyrus. I don't think he's so handsome, and I know Tova doesn't either. His face is too long, and his nose too pointy. But as I listened to him read the words of the *ketubah,* I began to change my mind about him. He must have known it was a difficult moment for Father. He couldn't read the marriage contract by himself or size up his daughter's suitor one last time. Guni's eyes were kind and gentle. His voice was soft but in command.

It was filled with respect for Father.

I looked over at Tova. I knew she'd seen the same thing. Her head was lowered, and her pale cheeks were flushed with pink. Zaccai looked with pride upon his son, and even Mother nodded her approval.

I feel better now. I don't know very much about men, but if Guni treats my father with such respect, I think he'll do no less for my sister.

It's Sealed with a Sip

Tova sat beside Father with her hands clasped in her lap. She watched with wide eyes while Zaccai handed his son a wineskin and a metal cup. Guni tilted the skin until wine squirted out. He held the cup up and recited the blessing: "Blessed are you, O Lord our God, king of the universe, who creates the fruit of the vine."

Guni tilted the cup to his lips and sipped from it. He held it out to Tova, and she took it from his hands. Father whispered into her ear, and she nodded. Guni waited with an anxious face.

Mother said that if the bride drinks the wine from the cup, she accepts the offer of marriage. From that moment on, she's bound to her suitor. Though they can't be together for a time, it's as though they're married. Only a decree of divorce can untie them.

Tova stole one last glance at Mother and Father and me. Then she lifted the cup to her lips and took a long, deep drink. Zaccai clapped his hands and shouted with delight.

"Now, Tova," Guni said. "I'll leave to prepare our wedding chamber."

I touched my chest and felt my heart knock against my ribs. I wasn't ready for Tova to leave just yet. "When?" I asked Mother. "When will the wedding be?"

Guni overheard, and he directed his attention toward me. "No one can answer your question, Alisah. Not your mother or father or even me! I must first build a wedding chamber for your sister and me. It must be built according to my father's exact specifications."

Zaccai nodded in agreement. "When I see

that Guni has prepared a chamber worthy of Tova's presence, I'll give him my approval. Then he'll return for her."

The two men rose, but before they left, Guni put his arms around Father's shoulders. "Silas, I know you heard the provision of the bride-price in the *ketubah,* but I want to reassure you before I leave. A servant will arrive tomorrow. He's a fine shepherd, and he'll care for all of your flocks from now on."

They left, and Father gathered all of us in his arms. "He'll make a fine son-in-law, that Guni. I'll have nothing but the best for my Tova."

He tilted his head in my direction. "And for my Alisah, it'll be the same. Nothing but the best for her when it's time to wed."

Oh! I have written so much, my hand throbs! I see Tova walking toward me now. How unusual for her to come to me here in the grove! I must go. I can see by her face that she's troubled.

I'm Not Ready to Leave!

I'm back, and my stomach hurts with the news. Mother sent Tova to tell me that someone from Isaac's household will arrive in the morning for me.

"What?" I cried. "So soon? Why so soon?"

She rubbed her bottom and pushed the willowy branches out of her hair. "It's been planned for some time, but Mother didn't want to worry you. She knew you'd fret every second until you had to leave. Give me a moment to find a comfortable spot, and then we'll talk. This nest of yours wasn't made for a big bird like me."

I was nervous as I watched her smooth the dirt and push away the twigs. A pale blue veil covered her beautiful hair. "Why do you wear this?" I asked her. "We never wear veils in the camp."

"Oh, Alisah," she sighed. "It's been such a day for all of us. Such change. I must wear a veil now that I'm betrothed. It tells everyone that I belong to another."

I could feel the hot tears threatening to fall, and I pressed my eyelids together tight so they couldn't escape. I'm too old to cry.

"I know Guni said we won't know the day of the wedding, but when do you think it will be? What if I'm not here when you make your preparations? I couldn't bear it."

She looked at me with such sweetness that I thought I would cry for sure. I couldn't leave her. I couldn't leave Mother and Father. I wasn't ready to go yet.

"Not until the new year, at least," she reassured me. "That's what Mother said. You'll come back in time. I'm sure of it."

I put my head in her lap, and she played with my hair like she used to. "I don't want everything to change any more than you do," she told me. "I'm afraid just like you are. I don't want you to go, but both of us have to be strong. We have to do what's right to help Mother and Father."

Tova stayed with me for a little while. She stayed until I felt better. My stomach gnaws at me though. I must return to camp and pack my belongings. I don't have many, so it shouldn't take long.

I've discovered a secret that helps me not to cry. When I feel my eyes sting and prickle, I blink as fast as I can. It makes the tears retreat— sometimes. It's a good thing I've discovered this. I don't want anyone in Isaac's camp to think I'm just a child. I must not cry in front of them.

Sunrise

I'm waiting in my tent for someone from Isaac's household to arrive and take me away. Tova said I'm being too dramatic about it. "They're not taking you away!" she said with a light laugh. But I could see in her eyes that she was as sad as me. "They're just accompanying you to a place where you'll work for a time."

I looked at her and nodded my head. "They're taking me away," I repeated.

Everyone has come in to check on me at

least twice. I don't know why. I've reassured Mother and Father that I'm fine. I promised Tova that I would put on a happy face for them, and I'll continue to try my very best.

Last night I wrapped my belongings in my blanket. My blanket is the most special thing I own. It's striped blue and green, and I've had it since I was born, Mother tells me. I can believe it. It's threadbare in many parts where I've rubbed it between my fingers for so many years. The colors are bleached from the sun's hot rays, which dried it after many good washes in the springs.

Inside the bundle are two rolled tunics, an extra pair of sandals, and my metal drinking cup. My bed mat is rolled up as well and tied with a string. Mother came in as I was gathering my things. She knelt down beside me and placed a silver comb in my hand. There was a small pearl on either end of it.

I couldn't find my voice for a long time. I'd watched Mother run this beautiful comb through her thick black locks every evening for as long as I could remember.

I shook my head. "I can't take this from you. You use it every night."

"Alisah," she said, "love gifts are not just given to a bride. They can be given to anyone you love. I can't be with you for a time, just as Guni can't be with Tova. I want you to have this."

She pressed it deeper into my palm and closed my fingers around it. "Your father gave this to me when we were betrothed. Every time you comb your lovely hair, think of me. We'll be together again soon."

I blinked as hard as I could and buried my face in her shoulder so she wouldn't see me. "I will," I told her. "I can never forget you."

Tova presented me with the pale blue veil she wore yesterday when we were in the tamarisk grove together, and Father gave me a single red ribbon. He held it up in front of me as I sat in my tent. Just then, a warm desert breeze pushed the tent flap open. The ribbon blew from his fingers into my lap.

"Alisah," he said. "When you were born, I

hung this red ribbon over your bedding. Our people have always believed that red ribbons ward off the evil spirits that try to take a baby's life. The color red is that of life-giving blood."

I rubbed it between my fingers. It was worn, like my blanket. "I know it was Yahweh, not this ribbon, that protected you," Father continued. "He will be your protector when you leave me. It's all I have to offer you, but my gift comes from my heart."

I'm wearing Tova's blue veil on my head, and Father's red ribbon is tied around my wrist. My mother's beautiful silver comb is packed inside my bundle.

Oh no! I just heard the bellow of a camel and the dry timbre of a traveler's voice. It's time for me to go. Dear friend, I'll leave you behind in the safekeeping of my mother. I'll begin a new diary as soon as time permits me to write again.

Diary Two
Beer Lahai Roi

1986–1985 B.C.

Journey to My New Home

We've traveled from sunup to nearly sundown, and I'm weary. There's much to tell though, and if I wait too long to write, I'll never remember all of it. I'll go back to this morning where I left off.

I heard the bellow of the camel and left my tent to find a boy waiting beside two crouched Arabian camels. He was slight and skinny, not unlike our goats. His eyes were very dark, and his hair reached his shoulders in long curls. I saw my mother's eyebrows shoot up in surprise. I looked around but could see no one else. Where was the person with the voice I had heard while I sat in my tent? Mother shrugged her shoulders when I looked at her.

The boy came forward. "My name is Crispus, servant of Isaac and Rebekah. I've come to escort Alisah to the household of my master and mistress." I was sure he couldn't have been much older than me, but his voice was deeper than I'd expected. It *was* the traveler's voice I'd heard.

"I'm Alisah," I said. I tried to fill my voice with confidence, but I heard it waver. "I'm prepared to leave."

Crispus held the reins as I climbed onto the camel's humped back. At the boy's command, it heaved its great body up with a loud snort. He tied my bundle and my bed mat to the camel's side and then climbed on his own camel. Without so much as a word, he began to move away from the camp. I had no choice but to follow him, swaying from side to side on the enormous beast.

The sun was rising in the east, and the doves cooed in the still air. I should have been gathering water from the well with Tova, tending to Father, or helping Mother gather more wood for the fire. Instead, I rode into the desert to a home that was not my own.

I left my family for the first time in my life, and I didn't look behind me. Hot tears burned my eyes and splashed onto my hands. I was ashamed of myself, and I didn't want anyone to see. Mostly, I couldn't bear to see my beloved ones fade away in the distance.

Out of the corner of my eye, I saw a man head toward our camp. He wore a shepherd's cloak and carried a staff. His sandals kicked up small clouds of yellow dust as he walked. I knew he must be the servant Guni had promised Father. I felt an unexpected wave of gratitude for the man my sister would marry.

The sun smoldered over my right shoulder throughout the first half of the day. The perspiration on my skin evaporated, and it felt dry and scratchy like tree bark. I drank frequently from my skin of water. Father had warned me about the importance of drinking enough.

"You aren't accustomed to traveling without your mother and father to take care of you," he'd said. "We won't be with you to warn you to drink water. The desert is a silent killer. You'll drop dead before you even feel the need to satisfy your thirst. Drink often, no matter what."

The Negev desert spread before me in shades of white, gray, tan, and brown. It was silent except for the occasional cry of the hawk or the melancholy whistles of Crispus. It was a sound that surprised me and brought me great comfort. Father had whistled until he lost his sight. He was depressed, and I knew that was the reason he stopped. Whistling meant peace and contentment to him, and he had neither.

I studied Crispus as we traveled southwest toward Beer Lahai Roi, my new home. His curls bounced on his shoulders as he sashayed on his camel. He must have felt my steady gaze, because he turned his head and said, "It's my curse."

I knew he spoke of his hair, and I was embarrassed that I'd been caught looking at him with such interest. It was very poor manners, and Mother would have scolded me on the spot had she been here.

"Please forgive me," I stammered. "I know better than to stare."

"It's all right," he laughed. "Everyone looks. I was born with a head full of curls. It's why my mother called me Crispus. My name means 'curled.' Oh, and in case you wondered, I'm not as young as I look. I'm fourteen."

We both laughed, and I knew from that moment on we'd be friends.

We stopped and made camp just a short while ago. There are a few acacia trees here, so Crispus said, "It's as good a place as any to stop in this desolate land." He's made a fire, and the twigs and dried leaves are crackling in the orange flames.

I'll be right back. It looks like he's rummaging for food!

The Night Settles upon Me

Crispus surprised me when he pulled out a pouch of dried fish. I told him I'd never tasted it before, and he said I was in for a real treat! He must have traded for it when the trade caravans came through. Fish isn't a common food in the Negev; the seas, the lakes, and the rivers are too far off.

He took an orange-brown chunk the size of my hand and placed it on a rock. He surprised me again when he began to beat it with a large stone.

I'm sure I amuse him, because he always laughs at the expressions on my face. He says I'm quite funny.

"I have to soften the flesh," he told me, "or you'd never be able to sink your teeth into it."

He beat it for quite some time, and I wondered if I really wanted to try it after all. If food needs to be beaten to death, perhaps it isn't meant to be eaten.

Crispus tested it with his fingers. When the flesh flaked off and fell to the ground, he declared that it was ready to eat. He pulled off a strip and gave it to me. It felt like leather that had baked in the sun for too long.

"Come on!" he said with his mouth full. "It's quite satisfying."

I decided to bite into it so he wouldn't think I was a child. I felt my eyes pucker at the taste.

"What do you think?" he asked, still chewing.

I nodded my head and smiled. I'd never tasted anything like it before. This piece of dried, salted fish was salty, pungent, and very strong. I finished my piece, not because I was fond of it, but because I still felt Mother peering at me, telling me to finish my food.

What a day of adventure this has been. I have a feeling it's just the beginning. Mother gave me the remainder of the figs and walnuts she brought out when Guni arrived the day before. Is it possible it was just yesterday? Crispus and I shared what remained of those. I've unrolled my mat, covered myself with my blanket, and rolled my extra tunic into a tight bundle beneath my head. I know I'll miss Mother and Tova in the early hours of the day, but my evenings belonged to Father and they'll be lonely without him.

I used to go with him to watch the flocks at night, when the sky was black and the moonlight silhouetted the sheep and goats. That was before he lost his sight. We would sit on a blanket spread out on the ground. My skin would prickle in anticipation as I watched him moisten his lips with his tongue and purse them together.

He'd be transformed into a magic snake charmer like those I've seen in the dirty marketplaces. His mouth would become his pipe, and our sheep would become his snake. Haunting melodies would swirl through the air and hypnotize our flocks until they were peaceful and sleepy.

"You're an interesting girl, Alisah," Crispus said.

I was so lost in my memories that I'd forgotten that he was a short distance from me.

"I've never known a girl who can read and write," he said. "I fear some of the girls in your new household will envy your talents."

"Or they'll find me silly," I told him.

"Only the silly ones will find you silly," he said.

Perhaps he's right. If Rebekah permits me, I could teach some of the girls to write. It wouldn't hurt them to put their thoughts down on paper. We shall see.

I'm ready to put my thoughts away and sleep now, dearest diary. I want this day to close.

The Stars Are Laughing

I can't sleep! The stars are amused, I'm sure of it. Each time I turn my eyes toward the sky, they wink at me. I've stirred the ashes and roused the flames. Crispus is asleep, and the fire shines on his hair. Thank you, moon, for glowing full and bright. At least I can write for a little while.

I laid my head down, but thoughts crept into my mind and swirled in such a way that I couldn't rest. They were unsettling memories of many moons past. I know why they come to me now. As I left this morning, I was reminded of the time, years go, when Father sent Mother and Tova and me away. I felt strange and afraid, and I didn't want to leave then, as I didn't want to leave this morning.

It was the season of locusts, and an *arbeh* plague was upon us. Father stayed behind to protect our home and our land from marauders, but in the end he gave in and followed us north.

It happened after three dry seasons. The earth was cracked and brittle. Tova and I would

49

crouch down to watch the little ants scurry out of the slivered ground in search of food. They returned like tiny soldiers, pulling a shriveled blade of grass three times their size or marching with tiny seeds tucked between their jaws. Sometimes we saved crumbs of bread and put them in their path when they returned from a foraging trip with nothing.

This last dry season was followed by a week of rain. That was when the trouble started. The cracks in the earth filled with water, but the packed dirt had become so dense that it couldn't absorb the rain. Puddles seeped beneath our tent walls and soaked our bedding.

When the rains stopped, green buds began to appear on the trees, and tender shoots sprouted from the land. Not long after that we saw the first yellow locust. It sprang from the bushes and landed close to my hands as I played outside one day. It was the length of Tova's pointer finger, and its back jumper legs were long and muscular. It had two sets of wings that twitched in the hot air. I laid my cheek to the ground and studied it. I was sure it was staring into my eyes, warning me of something, but Tova laughed at me when I told her this.

We didn't think too much about that locust, though it gave me an uneasy feeling in the hollow of my stomach. The next day we saw several more. The day after that there were so many that we captured them easily in our jugs. They littered the ground and crunched beneath our sandals as we walked.

Then a truly frightening thing happened. We were in the camp one day, close to the tents, when the sky to the northeast darkened. An enormous black cloud drifted toward us, shifting in shape as it rode on the wind. The noise it made was like a thousand horses pounding over the hills. It was deafening. I covered my ears, and Tova and I both ran to Mama and clung to her legs. She held her hand to her chest, and I heard her pray, "Mighty Lord, forgive us of our sins. Have mercy upon us."

The roar grew louder, but the sound of pounding hooves was replaced by the fluttering of a million wings. Papa was shouting to us, but to my ears his lips were silent. He ran to us and pulled us into a tent. Mama tied down the door flap, and she and Papa reached for items to place around the inside perimeter of the tent, anything to close the loose spaces and keep out the locusts.

Tova and I helped. We rolled up our cloaks and mattresses and pushed them around the edges. Pots and jugs were placed on top to secure them. We worked for many minutes to fortify the tent. When we had done all we could do, we huddled together and waited. The sun was hidden by the swarm of locusts, and the tent was blacker than the night. At least in the evenings we had a moon to give us light. On this night Papa wouldn't even let us burn a lamp.

The locusts began to drop from the sky. They fell on our tent like hailstones. For more than an hour, they pounded our tent walls. Then the beating of their wings quieted in an eerie fashion, and we heard them hum. Papa said he was sure there were many millions outside our shelter. He said every space of our land was covered with insects like a heavy, black blanket. They were devouring the plants and the leaves and the grass and any bit of vegetation within a five-day journey.

He prayed just as Mama had, and he also sang. All night long I drifted in and out of my dreams, listening to Papa's fervent prayers and the hum of a million insects. By the morning, they had all gone. Papa said they were swept away by a great wind sent by God. Not one locust had invaded our tent that evening.

Mama untied the tent flap, and I heard her gasp as she stepped outside. I hurried to follow her and froze. As far as my eyes could see, there was not a blade of grass or a leaf or a sprout of green vegetation anywhere. My tamarisk grove was a graveyard of skeletons. The trees waved their skinny brown "bones" in the morning air.

That was when Papa sent us away. He said we had to leave the devastation behind and travel until we found land that was fruitful, land the locusts hadn't ravaged. He said he would wait out the season, that he could survive until the grasses grew again. Then we could return, and our family would be reunited.

In the end he followed us. We stayed away only for a season, and until this morning I could say that we've been together ever since.

A New Morning

I awoke before dawn, wet with desert dew. It rarely rains in the summer months, but during the night the ground cools and the moisture in the air condenses into sparkling drops. On certain nights, when the air was thick and heavy, Mother left empty pots about the camp. When we checked them at sunup, they were filled with fresh dew.

Father always said Yahweh provides for his children in mysterious ways. The heavy dew waters the farmers' crops and nurtures the plants and trees of our wilderness area. He said it's another example of God's intervening hand.

I think about Father's words of wisdom now

that I'm away from him. How many times has he spoken of Yahweh and his goodness, Yahweh and his blessings, Yahweh and his sheltering hands? It has more meaning to me now that I'm away from my home. I'm glad his words are stored in my heart. They bring me comfort as I journey to a new place. I have more time to be lost in my thoughts now.

When Father began to lose his sight, I cried all the time. I didn't know what would become of us or who would take care of us.

"If Yahweh provides dew to water the plants," he'd said, "why do you worry that he won't provide for our needs? Do you think he loves you less than the wilds of the land?"

I must go. There's one more day of travel, and Crispus is impatient to move on.

My New Home

I write from my tent in my new home at Beer Lahai Roi. The tent is large, with several rooms divided by flaps of goat-hair cloth. Many girls, whom I haven't yet met, share it. Some of them have nodded to me, but most take no notice of my presence. Perhaps they're accustomed to new girls coming and going in the household.

It was another long day of travel, and we approached the camp as the sun melted into the earth. Enormous tents were stretched over poles like centipedes on the desert floor. I smelled bread and roasted meat on the breeze. I also heard the faint twang of the lyre. Even in my forlorn state, it was a welcome sight.

It's an oasis, my new home! I had no idea. We passed a pocket of palm trees heavy with dates. Crispus nodded toward an orchard of olive trees laden with unripe green fruit. "Those trees are very special to our people," he told me.

"Do you know why?"

I didn't.

"When Adam died, seeds were planted in his mouth," Crispus said. "The olive tree was one of three trees that sprouted from those seeds. The other two were the cedar and the cypress."

We passed a jungle of grape vines and crops of lentils, beans, cucumbers, leeks, and melons.

Immature figs clung to bushy trees with large leaves. Crispus reminded me that most of the fruit and vegetables wouldn't be harvested until next month.

"How do you know so much about the fields?" I asked him. He didn't have a chance to tell me

"Deborah is there," Crispus pointed to the tents as the camels brought us closer. "She's anxious to see you. I can tell."

A stooped figure emerged from the shadows of the camp and walked toward us on bare feet. The lamp she carried in her hand lit her face from below and bathed it in yellow light. Her eyes were blacker than the night, but they glittered and bore into mine just as they had five years ago.

I wanted to run and hide behind my mother's legs just as before, but this time I couldn't. My throat was dry, and my stomach quivered. I hadn't realized until now how nervous I was to see her again.

Without a word, Deborah took the reins

from my hand and whispered into the camel's ear. The beast dropped onto its front knees, propelling me forward until its rear legs folded beneath it.

Deborah surveyed me from head to toe. Her eyes took in Tova's blue head scarf with skepticism and passed over Father's red ribbon still tied around my wrist. Then she softened a bit and reached out a small, thin hand to help me from the camel. "I'm Deborah. I remember you well, child."

She was no taller than as I was, but there was nothing childlike about her. "Come," she said and turned on her heels. "You'll meet your mistress tomorrow. For now, you must eat and rest. I don't remember that you were a bundle of bones when I saw you last."

She said all of this over her shoulder as her gray braids bounced against her back. I turned toward Crispus, but he was already gone.

I'm happy to sit in my tent and be left alone for a while. A short time ago a young girl, not more than five or six, brought me my supper.

The household had finished their meal before I arrived, so I was grateful to be remembered. A small hand appeared in the tent and pushed open the flap. She was very pretty, with long brown braids and shy, gentle eyes. She held out a bowl and a spoon and returned a moment later with a cup of camels' milk before she disappeared again.

I've unrolled my bed mat, arranged my few belongings, and hidden Mother's comb beneath my tunics. Now I understand the meaning of *mattan*. These love gifts from my family have comforted me so. I'm grateful to have a piece of them with me.

The Next Day

Panic jolted me awake this morning. I sat up and expected to see Tova beside me, her black hair spread around her like a fan. Instead, I saw strange girls sprawled on their mats. It took me a full moment to realize where I was. I hope this doesn't happen to me again. My heart is still pounding against my ribs.

Last night I lay on my bed mat for a long time. I listened to the unfamiliar sounds of the camp. I thought I'd fall asleep at once, but I couldn't. I hope it doesn't take me too long to feel welcome and comfortable. I miss my safe and cozy home. I didn't realize until now how many things I've taken for granted in my young life.

Two new tunics were folded beside my bed mat when I awoke. I'm sure it must be the work of Deborah; I suspected she was unhappy with my attire when I arrived. They're a perfect fit and lovely too. One is the color of goats' milk, and it's striped with yellow and blue. The other is the color of a ripe, red date. It's my favorite, and I'm wearing it now. I discovered new sandals beside my old ones too. I suppose this is the reason Deborah sized me up so intently last night.

Just a moment ago a girl about my age offered some friendly conversation. At least it seemed friendly at the start. She shares the tent, and I felt her eyes on me for a long while before she spoke.

"You're the new nursemaid?" she asked. Her hair was a dull brown, and her eyes were small and narrow.

"Yes, I suppose so," I replied with as much lightness as I could muster. "Although I don't know a thing about being a nursemaid."

"Don't worry. Deborah will teach you everything you need to know," she laughed. "But I hope someone has warned you about her."

"Warned me? Warned me about what?"

"Oh, it's nothing to worry about," she said. "It's just that she's very protective of Rebekah and the twins. She can get a bit fierce at times. She doesn't want to share her duties, you know, but Rebekah insisted that she needed help. That's why you're here. It was at Rebekah's insistence, not Deborah's. She never wanted you here to begin with."

I didn't know what to say after that, so I said nothing.

"I'm Mary, by the way," she added with cheer. "I can be your friend if you want. I suppose you'll be in need of one."

I'm not quite sure what to make of Mary, but I can't sit here all day and fuss about it. I'm here now. Deborah was a bit gruff but not as sinister as Mary implied. I'll go look for her. I can't be idle any longer. Mother wouldn't be pleased about it.

Later

The camp was bustling with activity when I ventured out of the tent. I wandered without direction and envied everyone his or her appointed chores. I looked for Crispus's familiar face but to no avail. I don't even know where he is or what he does. How thoughtless of me, I realize now, that I hadn't even thought to ask. My thoughts had been of myself alone.

Mary disappeared after our conversation, but I found her outside, away from the tent, spinning flax. She held a sort of short stick with the flax wrapped around it in her left hand—a distaff, I think it's called—and a stone spindle in her right, and she wound the fiber from one to the other, twisting it along the way. The thread she made would be given to the weaver to make cloth.

I dislike spinning, and I dislike weaving even more. I don't like to sit in one place for long unless I can write. Mary looked up and gave me a little smile. She motioned for me to come over, but I shook my head and waved to her. I had to look for Deborah, but I'd also decided it was wise to stay clear of Mary for a time.

Several of the girls had just returned from the field with milk jugs balanced on their shoulders. I watched them work for a moment and was impressed. They seemed to have an efficient system worked out. The camels' milk was set apart; it could be used right away. Jugs of sheep's and goats' milk were set down in another spot to be churned into butter.

One of the girls poured that milk into a skin,

blew air into it, and shook it without mercy. The clear liquid would be poured off and stored in a separate skin to be used later, or they would use it to prepare food. The churned butter that remained in the skin would be heated with flour and spices, and the curds would be salted and eaten for breakfast or with the evening meal.

I heard someone call my name while I stood there. When I looked up, I was taken back five years to Abraham's funeral—"That's Rebekah, Isaac's wife," my mother had told me. The sun had shone on her black hair that day and reflected strands of blue silk. It did the same today.

Rebekah moved toward me on graceful, sandaled feet. "Alisah! Deborah told me you'd arrived. I've been so anxious to meet you. Do you remember me?"

I opened my mouth to answer, but before I could speak, a man appeared at her side. *"Shalom alechem,* Alisah. I'm Isaac." His silver hair and beard draped his head and chin in much the same way Abraham's had.

Rebekah studied me with pleasure in her eyes. "You've grown so much since I saw you last!"

Isaac nodded his head in agreement. "We're honored that you've decided to join our household. I'm sorry that your father, Silas, isn't well."

He was interrupted by the shuffle of footsteps, and we all turned to see Deborah. Her face was flushed, and she glared at me with the piercing black eyes I'd grown to dread. "There you are, child," she gasped. "I've looked all over for you." Her crinkled forehead and drawn mouth told me she was none too happy about it.

"Ah, dearest Deborah." Rebekah laughed and directed a wink toward me. "It's all my fault. I engaged Alisah in conversation. I couldn't wait to talk with her."

Isaac gathered Deborah in his arms, and the old woman's face softened at once.

After Supper

I followed Deborah around for the remainder of the day, and I learned much about her role as nursemaid. She told me it had expanded as the household grew through the years. She'd been Rebekah's nursemaid long before Rebekah married Isaac. Then she'd devoted herself to Jacob and Esau.

Now that the twins are twenty years old, she's become a matriarch in the household, one who is respected and even revered for her knowledge and wisdom.

To the younger children, she tells stories, makes up riddles, and sings songs. She teaches them to weave their cloth, bake their bread, and perform all the chores and duties that must be learned. When the children are finished with their chores, they're allowed their playtime.

There are rattles for the tiniest children to play with. I remember having one when I was very young. Mother has it now. She saves all our things in a special treasure box. When we're married and have children of our own, she'll return them to us. She says she'll add special things of her own to it. These are our heirlooms, she tells us.

My rattle was shaped like a spool, and it had tiny pebbles inside that made a wonderful noise when I shook it. I carried it everywhere. The rattle that Tova played with had pottery shards inside, and it tinkled more.

Deborah has taught all the children to play board games. There are clay boards and stone boards and tiny pieces that sit on top. The children know how to maneuver around the board with such skill that it surprises me. They try to win the other players' pieces, and sometimes they play for keeps.

Most of the young ones have made or found their own game pieces, and they tuck them away in pouches and hide them in their pockets. These pieces are a source of pride to them, and they are cherished. Some are tiny, smooth pebbles or small, conical stones. Some are bits of bone smoothed and polished to a soft finish or pieces of clay shaped by hand and baked in the sun.

I've heard of traders who sell play pieces made of ivory and ebony. And some pieces are fashioned from the shell of the abalone, which is lined with mother of pearl. Father said there are dice made of precious stones and gems that are nearly translucent. They glow with colored light when held up to the sun. I can't imagine such a luxury. Perhaps these toys belong to princes and princesses who live in palaces in exotic parts of the world. I'm certainly not one of those.

Many of the children here are content to play with clay horses in the grassy area beside the tents. Others run, jump, and tag one another. They race around bushes and over mounds of dirt to see who's the fastest. There's no end to the games they play.

To the older ones, even the grown men like Jacob and Esau, Deborah is a confidante, advisor, and friend. I didn't see a single person whose eyes didn't shine when she approached.

Several Days Later

I've developed a following among the littlest girls and boys. I think this is what Rebekah had hoped for, and it appears that Deborah is relieved. She has less patience for the little ones now. I like it this way too. The young ones are mostly sweet, and they're great fun.

The others, Mary included, look at me like I'm a thief and have come to steal from them. What they think I would steal I have no idea. I don't anticipate that I'll have many friends here. They're silly and trivial, and I have no patience for them.

Claudia is one of my favorite little ones. She's the pretty girl who brought me my supper the first night I arrived. Her father is one of Isaac's shepherds, and her mother died in childbirth. I've never had little ones to look after before. I was always the baby of my family. I feel grown up now, more like my sister, and I try to treat Claudia and the others with kindness and respect. That's the way Tova always treated me.

It was through Claudia that I learned the whereabouts of Crispus. I was teaching her and two others, Julia and Eunice, how to make fig cakes for the evening supper.

We poured a handful of almonds into a bowl and pressed them with a stone until they broke into small pieces. In another bowl, Eunice and Julia mixed walnuts and figs, and Claudia used all of her strength to grind them together. Each of them popped fruit and nuts into their mouths when they thought my head was turned.

Tova and I used to do that when we helped Mother fix supper. We stole bits of this and that when her back was turned. We thought she never saw us, but now I know she did, just like I see my little ones.

The girls rolled the dough between their palms until they formed little balls. They dipped them first into honey and then into the crushed almonds. "We don't have much honey left," Julia told me, "but Crispus will bring some when he gets back."

"Crispus?" I asked her. "Where is Crispus?"

"He's with Esau," she said as she licked her fingers.

"Where is Esau?" I hadn't seen Esau or Jacob since I arrived.

"Esau catches food for supper," Eunice told me. "Crispus helps him. They bring home wild meat."

"What about Jacob?" I asked them. "Where is he?"

"Oh, he takes care of the flocks," they explained. "And he also brings home the fruits and vegetables. Crispus helps him too."

So now I know why Crispus knew so much about the fields we passed outside of camp. He's a hunter like Esau, and he also helps Jacob with the farming.

I'm Suspicious of Mary

I was on the far side of camp today when I saw Mary enter our tent. She didn't come out for a long while, but before she did I saw her peer through the skinny opening between the flaps.

Her behavior is peculiar, and I'm growing more and more suspicious of her every day.

Until now, little diary, I kept you hidden in my rolled-up bed mat. Several times when I returned for you, I noticed that my mat wasn't arranged in the same way I left it. I suspect now that Mary has looked through the pages of this diary. I don't know that she can read, but from this moment forward, I'll keep you tucked into the pocket of my tunic. I must be more attentive to what goes on around me.

Crispus Returns—One Week Later

Esau and Crispus have returned with grand fanfare! Esau looks like I remember him, strong and rugged, only much taller now. An enormous antelope with broad, curved horns was strung on a long pole between him and Crispus. A dozen or more quail and turtledoves hung from the pole as well. It was quite a catch, and Isaac greeted his oldest son with pride in his eyes. Little Claudia was right. Crispus carried a honeycomb dripping with sweet, golden syrup.

The children, especially the boys, gathered around the men and chattered with excitement all the way into camp. Rebekah greeted Esau in a quieter manner.

When Jacob arrived several hours later, she ran and flung her arms around him and led him into the tents. It's not hard to see that Rebekah favors Jacob and Isaac favors Esau. It makes me feel sad. I wouldn't like it if Mother and Father showed favoritism toward Tova or me. I want them to love us just the same.

I've retired to my tent for the evening after the enormous feast. There was roasted antelope with figs, sweet bread with honey, wild gourds, and fresh fig cakes for desert. I haven't eaten this well for as long as I can remember, and I do feel guilty. I can't stop thinking about Mother and Father and Tova. I know Guni gave Father more flocks, but I'm still concerned about them.

I talked to Crispus about it after dinner, and he made a kind suggestion. "Allow Isaac to pay you in provisions instead of wages, and I'll bring them to your family. Esau and I must head out in a few days anyway. We have to catch and dry as much meat as possible before the fall harvest. We won't have time to leave as often then."

I think it's an excellent idea. I can enclose a letter to them as well, and Crispus can bring me news from home. He's a true friend, and I'm so grateful to him. I'll talk to Rebekah about it tomorrow. I've just said a prayer of thanks to Yahweh for my many blessings.

I Have Found a Field of Treasures

I supervised the little ones while they gently scraped the honeycomb. The syrup dripped into a tall clay jar with a slender neck. To my surprise, they led me to the field behind the tents where they pushed away the dry grasses and sticks and uncovered a row of large, smooth rocks.

They pulled away one of the rocks, and when I peeked inside I saw stacks of slender jars similar to the one we poured the honey into. I lifted some out and saw that they were all filled with olive oil. Julia had been right. There was no extra honey stored in the bottles. Straw lined the bottom and the sides of the shallow hole in the earth.

Eunice noticed the glee in my eyes. "Don't you store your food this way where you come from?" she asked me.

"No," I said. "We never had so much food that we needed to store it like this."

"Well, you can't tell anyone about this place," Claudia warned me. "Deborah told us that. She says we have treasures in the field and if we boast about them, a robber might come and steal them away."

I told the girls that Deborah was right. Before we left, they lifted away the other rocks and showed me where the grain was stored as well. These holes were much deeper and were plastered with a mixture of mud and straw to keep away the vermin. There must have been several homers of both wheat and barley grain— enough to last the whole winter, to be sure.

The Washing

I took the three girls to the well to draw enough water to wash some clothes. I've learned that the best way to teach them is to demonstrate just once and then allow them to try it on their own. I filled a large basin and dropped in a single white tunic.

"Now," I told them, "the next step is to mix a bit of animal fat with a handful of plant ashes and rub it into the soiled clothes." I showed them the goop in the small bowl, and they each made a face. I noticed two stains and began to work on those areas.

"Use two sticks," I continued absently, "and beat the clothing just like this."

I realize now, as I write, that I mimicked my own mother's words when she taught me to how wash clothes when I wasn't much older than these girls.

I beat the tunic clean, and the agitated water turned a murky brown. Tova used to say I was strange because I enjoyed cleaning clothes, but I feel a deep satisfaction when I scrub away the dirt. It's also a nice time for me to be lost in my daydreams.

That's what happened this time too. I was so absorbed in my thoughts that I forgot about the girls. When I looked up, Claudia was on her back, asleep, and Eunice and Julia were playing with dirt and grasshoppers.

I rinsed the tunic in a basin of fresh water, shook it fiercely so it would dry with few wrinkles, and hung it on a branch to bleach in the sun.

"When's lunch?" asked Eunice.

"Yes, my stomach is grumbling," echoed Julia.

Claudia sat up, startled from her nap. She blinked her eyes twice. "That tunic looks very nice on that branch," she remarked.

Oh, dearest diary, I'll have to rethink my lesson plans for the next few days. This isn't going to be as easy as I thought. The girls are eating their noontime meal, and I've escaped to my tent to rest in the shade.

Rebekah called to me a short while ago. I

didn't have to ask her about my wages or the provisions Crispus suggested. She already knew about it. She came in and sat on my bed mat, and we talked for a long while. Tova was right about her and Isaac. They're kind and gentle souls, and they serve Yahweh. Rebekah has also surprised me with her loving, generous spirit.

"You don't have to worry about your mother and father," she told me. "We'll take care of them. Crispus and Esau will deliver many provisions to them. It's the least we can do."

Rebekah has the generous heart of a servant, even though she's the wife of the son of Abraham! The generosity she shows toward my family has humbled me. I'm selfish and spoiled compared to her. Tova, on the other hand, is very much like Rebekah. My sister will devote her life to Guni so she can help Mother and Father. All I've done is complain. My heart sags with shame. I have much to think about.

Crispus and Esau Have Left

By the time I awakened, Crispus and Esau had tied the last of their bundles to the camels. Their quivers hung over their shoulders, and they gripped their long bows in their hands.

Rebekah put her arm around me and pointed to the sacks. "There's wheat, lentils, salted meat, dried figs, nuts, and even fresh honey," she said with pride. "In a few months, the men will bring them the fruits of the fall harvest as well."

I hugged her and blinked hard to stop the flow of tears. "Oh, Rebekah, they'll love it."

I tried to imagine the look on Mother's face when she opened the sacks. Wheat! Mother and Father haven't had wheat for as long as I can remember. Barley, yes. Millet and spelt, yes. But we couldn't afford wheat.

I remembered the letter in my hand and ran up to Crispus. The scrap of papyrus was rolled up and tied with a piece of string. Mother had never been taught to read, and Father couldn't make out the letters anymore, but I knew Tova could share the letter with them.

Dearest Mother, Father, and Tova:

Crispus and Esau were kind enough to drop off these provisions for you during their hunting trip. As you will see, Rebekah and Isaac were very generous. There will be more to come in the next few months. Who knows, perhaps I can work out a visit sometime.

I hope you are well. I've been worried about you. I feel better now that all of this food is headed your way.

I'm fine, so there's no need to fuss about me! I have three little girls that I tend to quite a bit. They've grown attached to me already and I to them. Claudia is my favorite. She's very sweet. Julia is the smart one, and Eunice is quite playful. Deborah oversees the older ones, which is fitting. She's very devoted to the family, but I suppose you already knew that!

Crispus has proven to be a good friend. I'm thankful that he's here, although he's gone quite often in the fields with Esau. Rebekah and Isaac are kind and generous and loving, and I've learned quite a lot from Deborah. Rest assured, I'm in good hands here.

I miss you, and I can't wait to see you again. My mattan *is dear to me, and I'm grateful that a piece of each of you is so near. I love you with all my heart.*

Your loving daughter and sister,

Alisah

"We'll deliver your love," Crispus said and tucked the letter into his sack. Then they were gone. Today I've learned the true meaning of giving. I felt so good when Crispus and Esau left to deliver the provisions. It's a far better feeling than I ever had when I received something. It's deeper and truer and infinitely more satisfying.

I've Been Cursed!

Oh! I can't believe what has happened to me! Two days have passed since I last wrote, dear friend, because I've taken ill. I'm in recovery, but Deborah says I'm confined to my bed mat for several more days. It seems I've been stricken with *ayin hara*—the evil eye!

When Tova and I were very small, Mother told us, "Never envy what another person has. If you look at someone for too long with envy in your eyes, you can give them an illness called *ayin harah*."

The evil eye, she said, isn't passed on intentionally, but that doesn't make it any less dangerous. You must get help right away, or you may never recover.

"But what if someone pays us a compliment and is envious of us?" Tova asked many times. She was frightened by the notion, but I never was. I never believed it could happen. After all, no one in our family ever had the evil eye—until now.

"Then you tell that person to touch you or spit on you right away," Mother answered. "It will help diffuse the compliment, and the evil eye won't take hold of you."

Two days ago my insides became loose and squeamish and my head felt light. Deborah was with me at the time. She said the color drained from my face, like water from a jug, and I turned pale and pasty. She took my arm and tried to help me to my tent, but before we had taken three steps, I vomited. My head throbbed, and I was unbearably sleepy.

I was resting on my mat when I heard her confer with Rebekah outside of my tent. Their voices were low, and I could see their silhouettes through the wall of the tent.

"It must be *ayin harah*," Deborah told her. "No one else in the camp is ill. It came upon her too fast. I recognize these symptoms."

"Ayin harah!" Rebekah exclaimed. She pushed open the tent flap and sat down beside me. "My goodness, Deborah, you must act at once. She's burning with fever."

I felt the salty beads of sweat slide down my cheeks and neck in rivulets.

Deborah slipped away and returned moments later with a basin of water. Rebekah dipped a cloth inside of it and pressed it against my forehead and over my cheeks. I was cold from the inside out, and I shivered uncontrollably.

She pulled the blanket up to my chin and tucked it around me. "What else can be done?" she asked the nursemaid. "There must be more we can do for her."

"We must first know for certain if it is the evil eye," Deborah replied. "There's only one way to find out."

She moved the basin and set down a pan of water in its place. Above it, she tipped a small jar until a single drop of olive oil splashed into the water. "Now watch," she told Rebekah. "We'll see what form it takes."

The drop of oil floated lazily on the surface of the water. Minutes passed. I listened to the hushed voices drift from the camp. I knew that everyone must have heard the news by now.

Deborah's eyes didn't leave the pan. The yellow film began to drift, and all at once Rebekah's breath caught in her throat. The drop of oil had spread until it resembled the shape of an eye. I leaned over as far as I could and stared into the water. There was no mistake about it. It was an eye.

"*Ayin harah,*" Rebekah said under her breath. She reached for my hand. "Now we're certain it is the evil eye. What now, Deborah? What can be done now?"

Deborah lifted the jar above the water again. The oil fell into the pan, one glistening drop at a time. I leaned my head back again and closed my eyes. I heard the oil splash and listened as Deborah murmured a long and sorrowful prayer. Her voice dipped higher and lower with such a sweet resonance that it didn't seem possible that it came from the wrinkled, brazen woman by my side.

"There now," Deborah said to me. "Give in to your sleepiness. When you awaken, you'll find that your sickness is gone. You'll be weak for several more days, so you must stay in bed for that time. The *ayin harah* has left you."

Deborah was right. My strength hasn't returned to me yet. I will rest for a while.

I'm Still in Bed

The little girls come and go. I see their heads peek through the tent door, and I hear their giggles. Deborah has put them in charge of bringing me my meals. So far they've done a wonderful job.

Mary and the other girls who share the tent are nowhere to be found! I haven't seen them since I've been ill. I suspect they're afraid of *ayin harah* even though it isn't contagious. I've had plenty of time to ponder my condition, and I just remembered Crispus's words on the first night of our journey—"I've never known a girl who can read and write," he'd said. "I fear some of the girls in your new household will envy your talents."

Envy, he had said. The only girl who displays any sort of envy is Mary. She often stares at me while I write in my diary. She also said strange things to me when I arrived, not the sort of things I would tell someone if I was trying to make her feel welcome in her new home. I suspect that she rifled through these pages of papyrus as well.

Deborah asked me yesterday if there was anyone in the camp who may have given me the evil eye. I shook my head. "Well, there must be someone, child," she said. "The evil eye doesn't appear by itself. We need to find the person who made you ill and explain to them the evils of envy."

Perhaps there's a better way. I want to think on this a bit more.

An Evening of Stars and Stories

What a wonderful night it has been. Rebekah has retired for the evening and has left two clay lamps burning beside my bed. She knew I'd write to you before I fell asleep.

She came in this evening as I combed my hair. "Alisah! What a lovely comb. It becomes you." She sat beside me on my mat.

I ran my fingers over the length of the silver comb and touched the pearls on either end. "My father gave it to my mother when they were betrothed. She gave it to me when I went away. She calls it a love gift."

Rebekah smiled. She reached up and touched the small golden ring that hung from her left nostril. "This was a love gift. It was given to me by Eliezer, on behalf of Isaac and his father Abraham."

Two gold bracelets hung from her delicate wrist. They tinkled together as she held up her arm. "These too. I've never taken them off."

I thought of Tova and Guni, and I sat up on my mat. "How did you meet Isaac?" I asked her suddenly. "Was he chosen for you?"

Rebekah laughed. "No, he wasn't chosen for me. I was chosen for him. Abraham was old, and he had all the riches a man could ask for, but he didn't have a wife for his son Isaac. He told his most trusted servant, Eliezer, to leave at once and find a good wife for his son. He told him, 'Yahweh, before whom I have walked, will send an angel with you so your journey will be a success.'"

An angel! I couldn't speak for a long moment. I thought about this angel who accompanied Eliezer as he traveled. "How did Eliezer know where to go?" I asked. "Did the angel direct him?"

"Well, Abraham had certain requirements, I was to learn much later." she replied. "He told the old servant that Isaac's wife must not be the daughter of a Canaanite. He would have to leave the land of Canaan and travel to Aram Naharaim, the country of his birth. He wanted Eliezer to find a wife among his own relatives.

"That very day, the devoted servant loaded up ten camels and left Hebron. He traveled for many days, and he was weary and thirsty, but he didn't stop until he came to a particular well. It was on the outskirts of the small village of Nahor, in the land of Aram Naharaim."

"Rebekah!" I exclaimed. "Did the angel direct Eliezer to this well?"

She gazed at me. "Listen to the rest of the story, and you'll have the answer to your question.

"The sun was low in the sky, and Eliezer commanded the camels to kneel down by the well. He lifted his hands toward heaven and offered a fervent prayer to Yahweh.

"'Oh, LORD, God of my master Abraham,' he cried, 'give me success today and show kindness to my master, Abraham. See, I am standing beside this spring, and the daughters of the townspeople are coming out to draw water. May it be that when I say to a girl, "Please let down your jar that I may have a drink," and she replies, "Drink, and I'll water your camels too"—let her be the one you have chosen for your servant Isaac.'"

The tent flap swayed, and Deborah slipped in. The light was dim, and I was grateful for the two lit lamps she carried. She placed them on either side of my mat.

"Unaware of what had just taken place,"

Rebekah continued, "I hurried from my home to the well. I wanted to fill my jar and return before darkness fell. I passed an old man and many camels, but I paid them little heed; thirsty travelers were a common sight there. As I turned to leave, I heard the shuffle of footsteps behind me. A deep, weary voice called out, 'Please, give me a little water from your jar.'"

Rebekah paused, and I sat up farther and leaned closer. The tent was very quiet. I could hear our breaths mingle together as we waited. "Did you hear Eliezer's prayer as you walked up the path?" I asked her.

"Oh, no," she responded. "But when I heard his voice call to me, I felt my heart stir within me. The sky was growing dark. I was in a hurry to get home, yet I lowered my jar and told him, 'Drink, my Lord.'"

Deborah moved from the shadows and sat down beside Rebekah. Her blue veins were plump in her thin, clasped hands, and her black eyes glittered as they bore into mine. "You know what she did then, don't you, child?" she asked.

"She offered to water Eliezer's camels."

"That's right." Deborah said. "She took her pitcher and emptied the water into the trough beside those ten beasts. Then she went back to the well, filled up her pitcher and dumped the water into the trough again. She did that over and over again until those camels were drunk with water. She had no idea that I'd followed her and watched from the path."

They rose to leave with a promise to return the next evening and tell me more. As Rebekah was poised in the doorway, she said to me, "Alisah, I wasn't able to water those camels with my own strength. It would have taken at least ten of me to draw enough water to quench the thirst of as many camels. Yahweh lifted my arms and enabled me to care for man and beast."

The Next Day

At last! I'm allowed to venture into the camp. I'm not accustomed to being entombed in my own tent! I didn't sleep well last night. I relived

Rebekah's story in my dreams, and then I awakened with thoughts of Mary. By the time the first rays of light broke the shade of night, I had my plan.

I found Mary by the campfire. She was kneading dough for the early bread, but she kept her eyes averted when she saw me approach.

"It's all right," I said. I bent low so I could whisper in her ear. "I haven't said a thing to Deborah, although she asked me outright who gave me the evil eye. I know it was you."

Mary froze for a long moment, and I saw a huge tear fall into the bowl. Her shoulders began to shake.

"Come on," I told her and took her trembling hand in my own. "Follow me."

I led her to a grove of trees, far enough away that no one could hear us. "Don't be angry with me," she sputtered. "It's true that I was envious of you, but I never meant to give you *ayin harah*."

I told her that it was all right and that the real reason I'd come was to offer an apology to her.

Her cheeks were wet, and her eyes were red. "An apology? You? For what?"

"I wasn't kind to anyone when I arrived," I admitted. "I didn't want to be here. I knew that most of you girls couldn't read or write, but I went ahead and pulled out my papyrus and pen in front of you anyway. I was arrogant. I'm sorry, Mary."

We talked for a long time beneath that grove of trees. I told her about Father's illness and how poor we'd become as a result of it. I shared about Tova's betrothal and the real reason I'd come to Beer Lahai Roi.

Then I asked her if she'd like to learn to read and write.

"You'd do that?" she asked me with startled eyes. "After what I've put you through? After the mean things I said to you when you first arrived?"

I told her that if she learned to read and write, she wouldn't feel envious of others who could. Mary didn't say anything for a while. She stared at her small, sandaled feet and sighed.

"I have to tell you something," she said in a small, tight voice. "I looked through your things. I didn't take anything—I never would— but I did look."

Her face was flushed with humiliation, and I felt sorry for her. She didn't have to tell me, and I was impressed that she did. I didn't tell her that I had already guessed it was her. She felt bad enough. We walked back to the camp hand in hand.

"You're different from all the other girls, Alisah," she told me "You're kind and gentle like Rebekah. She believes there's just one god. Do you believe that too?"

Mary's question took me back several years to a time when I asked Father about the same matter. His reply to me was, "Yes, I believe only in Yahweh. It's what father Abraham taught us long ago." That's the same reply I gave Mary. She looked at me quizzically. "What about the moon god who measures the time and regulates the tides?"

"Yahweh created the moon. Surely he can

manage the time and the tides," I told her.

"The sun god?"

"Yahweh."

"The storm god?"

"Yahweh. Mary, Yahweh alone oversees the moon, the sun, the stars, and everything below. He is God of all."

We agreed that we'd begin our lessons the next day. Mary has been transformed, and once again I feel a deep fulfillment inside of me. I've grown so much. I'm no longer the child I was when I began my journey.

The Month "to Shout for Joy"

The scorching desert heat has left us! Soon it will be time to gather in the fruits and vegetables. It's a month that means "to shout for joy" because of the rich fall harvest and grape vintage.

Last evening Rebekah and Deborah were true to their word. They came to my tent just as an early storm blew in from the west. Cool sea winds thrashed our camp for hours. They tugged at the wooden toggles of the tents and threatened to set them free. I was grateful for Rebekah and Deborah's company.

Mary sat in a corner, quiet as a desert mouse. She was too shy to come closer to us, but she listened with attentive ears as Rebekah and Deborah picked up where they'd left off.

"Listen well, child," Deborah told me. "When Rebekah finished watering those ugly beasts, that old servant pulled a golden nose ring and two gold bracelets from his pocket."

My eyes shifted to the jewelry Rebekah had shown me the night before. I tried to picture her face when she saw them for the first time. She would have been twenty years old at the time.

"'Whose daughter are you?' he asked her, 'Please tell me, is there room in your father's house for us to spend the night?'

"When Rebekah told him about her family, Eliezer dropped to the ground, right then and there, and began to worship the Lord. With his face in the dust, he cried out, 'Praise be to the LORD, the God of my master Abraham, who has not abandoned his kindness and faithfulness to my master. As for me, the LORD has led me on my journey to the very house of my master's relatives.'"

The sky flashed white with lightening, and the tent was lit for a brief second, illuminating Deborah's face like an apparition. Mary jumped up and scurried to my side, and we buried ourselves in a soft, woven blanket.

"That night Eliezer met Rebekah's family," Deborah continued, her face shrouded in shadows once again. "When he told them his story, her brother and father knew at once that it was arranged by the Lord. 'Here is Rebekah,' they said. 'Take her and go and let her become the wife of your master's son, as the LORD has directed.'

"Eliezer fell to the ground again. He worshiped the Lord with such might, the walls of the tent billowed with his breath. Then he went to the camels and untied bags of gold and silver jewelry, exquisite silk shawls, and embroidered veils the likes of which I've never seen. He gave these gifts to Rebekah and laid other costly gifts at the feet of her brother and her mother."

I was reminded then of Guni's gifts to my sister—the ivory hair comb and the golden hairpin encrusted with jewels. There were the cattle he gave to Father and the servant he sent over the next day. The presents weren't as lavish as those presented to Rebekah, but it was the most Zaccai and Guni could afford to give. To Tova and Mother and Father, they're priceless treasures.

"At sunrise," Deborah continued, "Eliezer was prepared to return home. When Rebekah agreed to leave with him at once, her family gathered near and said a beautiful blessing over her: 'Our sister, may you increase to thousands upon thousands; may your offspring possess the gates of your enemies.'"

"Deborah and I and several of my maids mounted Abraham's camels," Rebekah said, "and we left with Eliezer. I left my home forever that day."

I searched their faces and waited for one of them to continue, but neither said a word. "Rebekah!" I cried. "You'd never met Isaac, and yet you agreed to marry him?"

"Yes."

"Did you even know where you were going?"
I asked.

"No," she replied. "I had no idea where my
new home would be. Alisah, do you believe the
angel of the Lord directed Eliezer to that well?"

"Yes," I said. "I do believe that."

"Well, I believed that too. It was enough for
me to know that Yahweh had chosen me. When
the Lord calls, you must heed his call. There is
no time for questions, only action."

For the first time in weeks, my eyes prickled
and burned. I blinked as hard as I could, and
through my veil of unshed tears, I saw a smile
stretch across Deborah's leathered face. She put
her hand over mine. "Sleep, child, and you as
well, Mary. Tomorrow is another day."

I pushed my blanket out of the way and sat
up. "Wait! What happened next? When did Isaac
see Rebekah? When did . . ."

It was too late. They were gone. The wind

blew open the flap, and Mary ran to tie it down. I lay back on my mat and listened to the raindrops tap the roof. I heard them slide down the sides in cool sheets.

"Do you believe that?" Mary whispered to me in the dark. "That God directs our path and calls us?"

No one could see now, so I let the tears flow. I sniffed quietly before I answered her. "Yes," I told her. "I know now that it's true. Some people, like Rebekah, follow God's call with gladness. Other people, like me, ask every question they shouldn't. They go with heaviness and resentment in their hearts."

We were quiet for a long time. I knew Mary must have known I was crying, but I didn't care anymore. I'll never forget the next words she spoke to me.

"Alisah," she said, "if it's true what you say about God, then don't you think he called you here to teach you the very lesson you spoke of? Perhaps instead of feeling bad because you let God down, you should rejoice because he loved you enough to call you, lead you, and teach you."

One Week Later

I'm worried sick about Crispus. The rains continue to pummel our camp every day, and still he hasn't returned with Esau. It isn't uncommon to have an early storm or two, but the rainy season shouldn't be upon us for another month. The earth, dry as bone just a week ago, is covered with dirty puddles. Pitchers and basins, littered across the camp, collect the rainwater. There is one convenience though: We no longer have to draw water from the well.

The rains let up for a while each day, and during that time we hurry to fix the meals and complete our chores. Jacob comes and goes with the flocks, but it's obvious to me that he's happiest near his home among the tents. He's a quiet, contemplative man and not given to idle conversation. Isaac paces the camp more often as the days go by. I can tell he's worried about Esau.

My lessons with Mary have gone better than I expected. In fact, she has an artistic flair that surprises me. She moves her hand with grace as she dips the reed into the ink pot and rubs it against the paper. We're practicing the characters of the alphabet, and she has almost mastered them with the smooth, deliberate confidence of someone who has years of experience!

The little girls, Claudia, Eunice, and Julia, are my most recent students. They're allowed lessons after they've completed their chores around the camp. They're more challenging than Mary and require more patience on my part. I'm already in need of more papyrus, and I fear that if I don't get my hands on some soon, I'll run out of room to write to you. Deborah promised me she would look into it.

I have a few moments to myself, and I'll use this time to take a walk among the trees. I did this yesterday, and I was transfixed by the watery wonderland I had entered. The dusty path that leads from the camp is now a muddy stream beneath my feet. Droplets of water cling to the deep green leaves of the olive trees and shimmer in the light. I can smell the wet earth. Imagine that!

Flocks of quail bob among the bushes, and doves scatter from their perches when I walk near. There are even the tiniest of pink and purple wildflowers sprinkled about with the raindrops. I love it.

By the way, I just offered a prayer to Yahweh. If Abraham could pray and ask for an angel to guide Eliezer, then why can't I ask the Lord to send his angel to guide Crispus and Esau to safety? I believe I can, and anyway, I just did!

Daybreak—A Cloud of Doves

As if I haven't learned enough about myself already, a new and unflattering quality has been brought to my attention. I'm arrogant. I realize now that I've always made judgments about people based on my first shallow observations of them. I did it with Guni, and now I can see that I've done the same disservice to Mary.

She's a truly wonderful girl, and she continues to surprise and inspire me each day. This morning a cloud of doves alighted on the path ahead of us and Mary disappeared into a storm of dust and feathers. When she emerged, she held a small, graceful bird between her hands. The beak of the dove was so slender, and its eyes were so kind and peaceful.

She said there are many dovecotes—homes built for large droves of doves—in places like Egypt and the lands east of us. They're tall, round towers built broader at the bottom than at the top. They resemble a honeycomb pierced with hundreds of holes. It's through these holes that doves enter to find their cozy nests.

The birds flock to the dovecotes in clouds of fluttering wings. Mary was reminded of them when the doves flew in front of us. The clouds are so immense that the sun is obscured until the birds settle into their retreat. Their cages are decorated with pearls and rubies as if the doves are kings and queens visiting their summer palaces.

The purpose of the dovecotes is not nearly so romantic. They are kept for the manure that's made from their dung. Still, when Mary told me the story, her eyes shined with tales of different worlds. Why did I think she was just a simple girl? She'd never been taught to write or read, but now I know that she's traveled much more than I've even dreamed. I have a feeling that these stories and many more will be preserved on paper once Mary has been schooled for a bit longer. It won't be long.

Two Days Have Passed

Oh, glorious day! My prayers have been answered. Is Yahweh trying to teach me, among many things, the importance and power of prayer? I'm sure of it, because Crispus and Esau returned just a short while ago, weary and soiled from head to foot but safe! And what an enormous catch they brought back: a huge hart, a gazelle, another antelope, and more quail.

"Esau!" Rebekah scolded when they arrived. "It's too much meat. What will we do with all of this?"

"First, we'll first have a feast, Mother, so you can celebrate our safe return," he laughed and patted Crispus on the back. "And then we'll dry the meat, salt it, and store it for the winter. What we can't use, we'll give away."

Isaac put his arms around Esau. Jacob watched in silence. "Why so quiet, brother?" Esau asked his twin with a twinkle in his eye.

"You're not happy to see me?"

"I'm delighted that you've returned without harm." Jacob's voice was dry and even. "Father would have been crushed had you not. Come. Let's get the meat into camp. We'll have to take care of it, or tonight the wolves will pay us a visit."

I watched them unload the game. The children were gathered around them again, jumping and giggling in delight. When the last of the meat was carried to the outskirts of camp, Crispus walked toward me. His familiar curls bounced upon his shoulders. I held my breath when I saw a tiny bundle in his fingers.

"This is for you," he told me and placed the package in my hand. "I bring you good news from your home. All is well in your household, and your mother and father were very pleased with your gifts."

I dropped it into my pocket to look at later when I was alone. "Father was all right, then?" I asked him.

"Your father was fine. So were your mother and your sister. They pestered me about your welfare, and I assured them that you're a disgrace to Isaac's household. A bitter disappointment!"

"Crispus!" I knew he was joking, but I pretended to be hurt. "Anyway, I'm not the only disappointment. We expected you back days ago, and everyone has been very worried about you."

He eyed the brown puddles on either side of us. "I see that you've had your share of bad weather as well. We hoped to return before the rains, but I don't have to tell you that they arrived early this year. We were caught on the other side of a wadi for many days. When we first crossed, it was a dry, empty gully. When we returned, it was a small, raging river. We didn't dare cross. Flooded wadis hide water demons deep inside. If you cross, they'll pull you under for eternity."

He wasn't joking anymore, nor was he trying to scare me. I've heard of these water demons before; Father warned me about them. The rains cause the wadis to swell to dangerous depths, though they look deceptively shallow. Tunnels spin beneath the surface and snatch the strongest swimmers, sending them to an early grave.

"You were very wise then," I told him. "It was better that you waited."

Crispus left to wash and change into fresh clothes. It was good that he did. I didn't want to tell him, but the rancid odor of dried blood and dead meat clung to his skin.

My bundle sits beside me, and my fingers twitch to open it. I'll write again soon . . .

Later

It's better than I had hoped for. Mother sent along her looking glass, a tiny square of shiny brass with a handle. If I hold the metal in front of my face, I can see just one eye reflected at a time! It makes me laugh and think of the many times I played with it as a child. It's another love gift from my sweet mother.

There's also a small sheet of papyrus, a return letter from Tova! Both the letter and the looking glass were wrapped in one of Father's cotton handkerchiefs. It's old and worn and smells just like him—musky and earthy.

Tova's letter is a pure delight. I'll share it with you:

Dear Alisah:

I couldn't believe it when Crispus and Esau arrived! We didn't expect them. Mother almost fainted when she saw all the food you sent. It was very generous of you. She said it was too much for you to send, but since you did, she's very happy! Doesn't that sound just like her?

She convinced Crispus and Esau to stay to supper. I've been excused for a time so that I can write to you before they leave.

I loved your letter. This time I had tears in my eyes! What did I tell you about Isaac and Rebekah? Do you remember? I told you that they were kind and gentle souls. I can see that you agree with me, and I'm so glad. I knew they'd take good care of you. I just knew it.

Father is fine, so don't worry about him. He misses you, but he feels better now that there are flocks in the fields again. The servant Guni sent over is a very competent shepherd. No worries there.

Mother is as busy as ever, and she keeps me busy. She's afraid that if I sit for too long, I'll be cursed with an idle spirit. So she fills my hands with work all day—and father's hands too!

I miss you, sister. I have no one to gather water with, no one to milk the goats with, and no one to pester! Truly, I miss your company. I know that you must be a light in Rebekah's household, just as you are in ours.

If you can come for a visit soon, I know that we'd all be so happy.

Keep us close to your heart.

Lovingly,
Your sister, Tova

Like I said, it was better than I hoped for. It's the first time I've ever been described as generous!

That Night—A Feast under the Trees

I thought Esau was joking when he mentioned the feast, but he wasn't. It seems that a feast is common after a hunt. It's the second one I've enjoyed since I arrived. Crispus found me not long after he had changed, and he handed me a large basket. He carried one as well.

"Come on," he said. "We have some harvesting to do before supper."

Two days have passed since the last rain, so the fields aren't as muddy as before. Crispus said it should be the last of the early rains. He led me to the vineyards, and I held the basket beneath bunches of round, purple grapes as he cut the wiry stems with his knife. I popped the loose ones in my mouth, spit out the thick skins, and swallowed the juicy pulp whole. Oh, the sweetness of it!

We left the vineyards and walked to a grove of sycamore fig trees. These figs, he told me, were cultivated year round, but they had to be tended with care. He reached into his pocket, pulled out a little knife, and slit the figs on one of the trees until the sap squeezed out of the tiny incisions. He said they'd ripen faster that way.

The next tree was already dripping with the ripe fruit, so I added those figs to my basket. We moved into the garden and scooped out several sweetly scented melons, ten cucumbers, and several leeks. The rest, Crispus said, would be gathered over the next week or two. This was just for the feast.

Rebekah and I worked side by side when I returned. We prepared a dish called *leben*. It's Father's favorite, and I couldn't stop thinking about him. How I wish I could have served it to him tonight.

I cooked wheat in a pot over a hot fire until little bubbles burst into a raging boil. Then I set it on a rock to cool and dry out in the sun while Rebekah cooked the quail in camels' milk. In the meantime, we skewered chunks of deer meat and roasted them over the open fire. The drippings fell into a little pot. The drippings were served with the meat and eaten with warm bread.

At the last minute the wheat was piled onto a large plate and the quail was arranged around the outer edges. The melted fat from the pot was poured into a small bowl and pushed down into the center of the pile of wheat. We scooped up the meat and wheat with our fingers and dipped them into the fat.

We passed around a bowl of camels' milk, and each of us took a sip and passed it to the person beside us. We enjoyed our meal beneath the arms of several large, shady trees. It was a perfect evening. Together with the meat kabobs and the fresh fruits and vegetables from the field, it was a delicious feast once again. I'm full, satisfied, and sleepy.

I've Learned to Make Papyrus Paper

Who would have thought? Mary and I were in the shade on the outskirts of the camp when Crispus surprised us. He dragged an enormous stalk behind him, taller than himself. Mary giggled when he presented it to me.

"Here," he said, beaming with pride. "This is for you. I found it on our hunt. I forgot papyrus grows in the marshes north of us."

"That's papyrus?" I asked him. I eyed the stalk with suspicion.

"Yes. Isn't it a beauty?"

"Umm. Yes, it's very nice, but what am I

going to do with it?"

He hesitated. "Well, Deborah said you needed paper. It's much less expensive if you make your own than if you buy it from Egypt's trade caravans. I thought your father might have taught you."

I shook my head. "I don't think Father knew how. He used to trade for the paper in better times."

"Oh!" Crispus said. "Well, it doesn't matter. I know how, and I can teach you."

And so, dear diary, we made papyrus paper for the remainder of the day. Crispus set the stalk down in a clearing, stripped off its rind, and cut the inner pith into sections the length of my forearm. We filled a basin with water and soaked the pieces until they were clear and flexible. Then Crispus sliced each piece lengthwise into thin strips and molded them into a square. Mary and I helped him lay the squares edge to edge to form a sheet. Then we laid other pieces on top in a horizontal direction.

"Now press hard!" Crispus said.

We laughed as we pressed and pounded and beat the sheets until the water was drawn out and the juice from the plant sealed the paper together. Crispus said the sheets will have to dry in the sun for several days. Then, we'll have to scrape and rub the paper until it's smooth enough to write on. What a lot of work. I had no idea.

Diary Three
Beer Lahai Roi and Beersheba

1985 B.C.

The Month "to Begin"

At last! I have new paper to write on! It's not quite as smooth as the paper made in Egypt, but I like it since I had a hand in making it. My last diary scroll is rolled up around a stick like the first one.

A new year is upon us already, and I can't help but think of Mother, Father, and Tova. I suspect I won't be able to visit before Tova weds this year. Since the last hunt, there hasn't been a moment for Crispus, or anyone else, to slip away and take me north for a visit.

First there was the harvest. Now the rain has softened the ground and made it possible to ready the soil and begin to plow. It must be done now so the seeds can be planted next month. There has been considerable tension between Esau and Jacob. When they disagree, and it happens often enough, Rebekah flies to Jacob's defense and Isaac sides with Esau.

It has bothered me since I arrived, and today I worked up the courage to ask Deborah about it.

It was mid morning, and the littlest ones were resting in the shade of their tents. Even though the worst of the heat is behind us, the sun is still intense at this time of the day. All activity is kept to a minimum, so it was an ideal time to talk to her.

I posed my concerns Deborah, and she smiled. I don't see her smile very often, so when she did it filled my heart with joy. Her smile meant approval, and deep inside I yearned for Deborah's approval.

"I wondered when the time would come," she said. "Are you ready to hear the rest of the story?"

I was confused. "I thought I had," I told her. "The other night, by the fire."

"Stories are never that tidy, child," she chided. "Not real ones."

She moved closer to me and spoke low. "Rebekah and Isaac were married, and Abraham was filled with the Lord's peace. They settled into their life and were very affectionate toward one another. By all accounts except one, they were very happy."

I didn't know if I'd heard Deborah right. "*Except* one?" I repeated. "By all accounts *except* one?"

"Yes, child. Incline your ear. Many suns and moons passed and still they remained childless. Rebekah's empty womb wounded her heart and caused her to suffer. Her greatest fear was that she wouldn't give birth to Isaac's son. With each new year, she cried tears of humiliation.

"Isaac heard his wife's pain and pleaded with the Lord to give them children. The great God answered his prayers, and after twenty long years, Rebekah discovered that her womb was full. Every day she ran her hand over her swollen belly and sang songs of joy.

"Until one day she felt a great disturbance within her. There was a jostling within her womb, which frightened her. 'Why is this happening to me?' she asked the Lord.

"No sooner had she finished her petition, than the Lord replied, 'Two nations are in your womb, and two peoples from within you will be separated; one people will be stronger than the other, and the older will serve the younger.'

"A few months later I stood at the foot of Rebekah's bed. A robust baby, covered in fine hair like a wild animal, dropped into my hands. That was Esau. Another baby, smooth and tender as can be, tumbled out behind him. His hand grasped Esau's heel. As you know, that baby was Jacob."

"His hand grasped Esau's heel?" I repeated out loud. "Deborah, is that usual for a baby to do that?"

"I'm an old woman, child," Deborah said, "and I've seen many babies born, twins included, but I've never seen anything like that. It was the beginning of the fulfillment of God's words to Rebekah, mark my words. Though Jacob was the youngest, he came out of the womb ready to supplant his older brother in one way or another."

Sometimes, Deborah told me, it's God's way to pass over the strong and the robust and choose the weaker, more tender things of the world.

"But I still don't understand," I told her.

"Why does Rebekah favor Jacob so? Why does Isaac prefer Esau?"

Deborah sighed. Wrinkle lines creased her dried face like a sun-baked raisin. I imagined she had spent many of her years fretting about Rebekah and the family.

"I can't give you an answer to that, Alisah, because I don't know. Perhaps Rebekah feels more tender toward Jacob because he's the youngest. Perhaps Isaac feels more pride in Esau because he's the inheritor of his fortune. Only the Lord knows.

"But I can tell you this. It was a dangerous thing they did, and it can't be undone. This house was divided the moment Isaac and Rebekah each foolishly attached themselves to one child. The full fruits of their actions have yet to be seen, and I fear they tread on dangerous ground."

My flesh prickled at her words. I shiver even now as I recount this story.

The Month "to Drop"

The days have flown by. Crispus and Jacob plowed the soil last month, and last week they dropped tiny seeds of barley and wheat into the hungry dirt. Now it's time to drop the rye, millet, flax, and vegetable seeds.

Esau still disappears for days on end and always returns with a rich bounty of game, most often venison, which is Isaac's favorite.

Since Deborah shared with me the nature of the twins' birth, my curiosity has peaked. Rebekah noticed. When Jacob and Esau were both in the camp one day, she sat down beside me.

She inclined her head toward Esau. "He's a man of the world. The Lord made him a hunter, and so he's learned to live by his wits. He isn't unlike Nimrod. Do you remember hearing about Nimrod?"

"Father spoke of him once or twice. He was a great hunter, right?"

"Yes. He was the son of Cush, Noah's great grandson, and he was famous for his hunting skills. Like Nimrod before him, Esau isn't happy unless he's on the hunt. Isaac often says his personality would make him both a gentleman and a soldier."

I nodded. "What about Jacob? What's he like?"

Her face lit with pride. "Oh, he's from a different world than his brother," she beamed. "He's not as remarkable as Esau, but he's very special in a quiet, dignified way. He prefers solitude to sport, and he delights in the mysteries of the Lord. He frequents the tents of Melchizedek the priest, where his pores absorb divine truths that even I can't grasp."

Still, the tension between the two brothers increases each day. I wonder about the "dangerous ground" Deborah spoke of.

Several Weeks Later

My spirit sags today. A sad drama has just unfolded. The cooler winds of the last few months have carried anxiety and disquiet into the camp.

The weight of it grew heavier and heavier each day as if a storm brewed on the horizon. As you probably guessed, that storm was between Jacob and Esau.

Crispus just relayed to me the events of the sad drama. He and Esau returned from another hunt just before noon. "We were hungry," he told me. "From an acre away, we smelled the most delicious stew. Our mouths watered. Esau in particular was weak with hunger. He eats very little when he's on the hunt, and I don't think he realized how weak he'd become.

"When we got to the camp, we discovered Jacob bent over the pot of porridge. Esau stumbled forward. 'Quick' he told his brother, 'Let me have some of that red stew! I'm famished!'

"Jacob looked at him with steel in his eyes. 'First sell me your birthright, brother.'"

"His birthright!" I gasped. Crispus nodded. The birthright is an esteemed and coveted honor, bestowed only upon the firstborn son of every family. That son is entitled to a double portion of the father's inheritance or wealth.

Also, when the father dies, the firstborn son inherits his position of authority within the household.

I realized at once the significance of the moment between the two brothers, and for the first time I understood the tension between them. All these years, Jacob has been jealous of Esau's position in the household and of his relationship with Isaac.

"He didn't sell it to him . . . Please tell me he didn't sell it to him," I cried.

"He did," Crispus said. "He was weak, and he just gave up. He told Jacob, 'Look, I am about to die. What good is the birthright to me?'

"Jacob took advantage of his weakened state and made him swear an oath. Esau had to sell his birthright on the spot in order to get a bit of bread and some lentil stew. He's disappeared into the fields, and I don't think we'll be seeing him anytime soon. He'll be back, but right now he's angry."

Sadness washed over me. "Does Isaac know?"

"No. He wasn't in camp at the time, and

Rebekah has warned everyone not to tell him. She fears it will crush him, and it very well might."

"I still don't understand," I told him. "Why would he sell his cherished birthright for a morsel of food? He can't ever get it back. It's gone for good."

Crispus told me that Esau underestimated Jacob. He'd grown accustomed to his brother's plain and quiet ways, and he wasn't prepared when Jacob showed a cunning and clever mind. Plus, Esau never treasured his birthright as much as Jacob coveted it. He didn't realize its value until it was taken from him.

I can't help but think of the dangerous ground Deborah warned of weeks ago when she relayed the story of the twins' birth. I feel a terrible injustice has been done, and I'm frustrated at the lack of judgment used by both brothers.

The household is very quiet right now. I found Deborah a short time ago, but before I could say anything, she took me aside and said in a hushed voice, "Before you render your judgment upon Jacob, remember one thing. Remember the words the Lord spoke to Rebekah before she gave birth: 'Two nations are in your womb, and two peoples from within you will be separated; one people will be stronger than the other, and the older will serve the younger.'

"I've told you before. No story is ever as tidy as it appears," Deborah said. "Does it appear that this was part of Yahweh's plan all along?"

I know I'll ponder these events for some time to come, and I may never understand their true significance in this lifetime. I've learned so much, and yet I fear I know so little. Deborah told me this is when wisdom begins to take hold of you.

Several Days Later

You'll never believe what has just happened—again! It seems I have news for you nearly every day, dearest diary. A servant was dispatched from Zaccai and Guni's household to bring me word of my sister's impending wedding. Tova doesn't even know yet, and I've sworn an oath not to speak of it to Mother and Father. Guni's arrival must be a complete surprise, but he was kind enough to give me enough time to return home before he arrives.

I talked to Rebekah right away, but it seems Isaac has already made the arrangements. Crispus and I will leave at sunup to begin the journey home. She said I should stay for a while and return when Father gives me his permission.

"It's good for you to have time with your family," she said. "You should have returned sooner, and I feel bad that you haven't. Enjoy your stay, and return when the time is right."

She pulled me to her and held me close for a moment. "You're a special child, Alisah, but you don't seem like a child anymore. Your mother and father will be pleased. You've matured into a fine woman since your arrival."

I still hear Tova's words—"Isaac is a *tamin*, a good and gentle soul, and so is Rebekah." She was so right.

Sunup

I'm waiting for Crispus to pack the last of the provisions for the trip, as well as the goods I'll bring back for Mother and Father. He whistles in a merry way. I think Crispus is similar to Esau. He's happiest when he's on his way to somewhere else.

Mary is teary eyed, and so are the little ones, Claudia, Eunice, and Julia. I've told them that I'll return soon, but it doesn't seem to comfort them. I don't want them to be sad, but deep inside I feel good that they'll miss me so much. I'll miss them too.

I gave Mary two assignments to work on while I'm gone. First, since she has mastered the characters of the alphabet, she must take my place and continue to practice with the little girls. She agreed. In fact, there was a sparkle in her eyes. Second, I gave her a small roll of papyrus and told her that I want her to begin her own diary.

"You may have trouble with a few of the

words," I explained to her, "but you'll get better if you practice every day. Soon, with your flair with the pen, you'll surpass me in your writing skills."

She hugged me so tightly that for a moment I couldn't breathe!

Deborah gave me a long, thin bundle wrapped in muslin and tied with a string. She told me not to open it until I was well on my journey. "I've grown fond of you, child," she told me before she turned on her heel and walked away.

Oh, it appears Crispus is ready to ride on. I must mount my camel and begin my journey home. I love those words—*begin my journey home.*

Late the Next Day

We've settled for the night beside the same acacia trees we found on our journey to Beer Lahai Roi many months ago. This time there's no salted fish, but there is an abundance of dried meat. The sky is clear and bright, but the air is much cooler than it was before. I've pulled my blanket over my shoulders and am sitting close to the fire Crispus has built.

Just a few moments ago, Crispus and I had a revealing conversation. He handed me a package of food, and I bit off a piece of meat and chewed it thoughtfully.

"Crispus, it hasn't been that long since I left my home, but it seems like so much has changed in such a short period of time. I don't feel like the same person I was when I sat here with you before."

He gazed at me with a soft smile. "That's because you're not the same person. The person who sat here with me the first time was just a girl. A selfish little girl."

My eyes grew big at his words. I felt a little pang inside of me, but I knew he was right.

"I can tell you that now," he said, "because you aren't the same person. You've matured into a generous, thoughtful young woman. You're like a seed that ripens with the seasons and emerges from the ground a seedling and then a sapling. In your later years, you'll be like a mature tree that has weathered the rains, the searing sun, and the frost."

"Rebekah is like that," I commented. "And Deborah even more so. My mother and father are that way too. Why are you so wise, Crispus?"

"I've had a good teacher in Isaac. He's his father's son, after all."

The wolves are howling tonight, so Crispus said he'd feed the fire through the night and keep watch.

Just this moment I remembered the bundle Deborah gave me before I left. You'll never believe what was inside! My very own wooden palette with four new reed pens and two ink pots! My name is even inscribed on it! How did she do this? Where did this come from?

My heart beats fast, and I must calm it down so I can sleep. I've been so blessed in recent months. I smile when I think of Crispus's words to me. It's the second time someone has called me generous. Rebekah taught me to give of myself, and to her I'll always be grateful.

Back to My Home in Beersheba!

You'll never guess where I am right now! Well, maybe you will! I'm in my own tent, curled up on my bed beside my dearest sister. I think she knows I'm writing about her, because she just looked up at me and smiled. My heart is filled with such gladness, I think it will burst. It feels as though no time has passed, and if weren't for the change in me, I would think I'd never left.

We arrived hours ago. I saw the camp from several acres away, and I couldn't stop smiling. The wind was kicking up a thin veil of yellow dust, so I thought there was a good chance they wouldn't see us until we were upon them.

I was wrong. Father heard us before we were visible, and he stood at the entrance to the camp, his ear inclined in our direction. Mother spotted me first, and she held her hand to her chest and froze.

She ran toward us, stopped, and began running again. I saw Father's sun-browned cheeks stretch to reveal his gap-toothed smile. I scanned the horizon in search of Tova but didn't see her anywhere. My heart dropped, and I wondered if we were too late, if she was already married and I'd missed her.

Then she came around the tents, dropped her water jugs when she saw us, and ran. She held Father's arm as they waited for us.

We embraced for several moments, all four of us locked together. Father turned toward Crispus and apologized.

"Forgive our ill manners," he told him. "As you know, this was the first time Alisah has ever been away from us. Come. You shall have supper with us and spend the night. You can start back at sunup if you please, when you are well rested and well fed."

We walked toward the camp hand in hand, and I jumped when Mother pinched the back of my arm between her fingers. "Aha! You've grown fatter! You'll make a nice wife someday if you keep this up."

Tova is signaling to me that she's ready to snuff the lamp and go to sleep. Tomorrow is another day.

The Next Day

I've snuck away for a few precious moments and returned to my special spot in the tamarisk grove. All is well! I'm at peace again! My nest was messy with leaves and sticks, and I had to clear it out, but it's comfortable now. It's a strange feeling to leave my home and then return to it when so much has changed. I know this is still my home and always will be to some degree, but I'm no longer the child who used to inhabit it.

I feel sad when I think my childhood is slipping away, but I also feel anticipation and excitement about my future. Who will I marry? Where will Yahweh lead me?

Crispus left before the sun greeted the day. I was sad to see him go, and that surprised me.

I've grown dependent on his friendship in recent months.

"You'll come back, won't you?" he asked me. "Deborah has grown quite reliant upon you. Rebekah too."

I laughed. I know he'll miss me too, but he didn't know how to tell me so.

"Yes," I told him. "Make sure you reassure Deborah and Rebekah that I will return." He blushed then and rode off.

Mother and I spent the morning preparing Tova for Guni's arrival, though my sister doesn't agree with it. "Why now, Mother?" she complained. "We don't even know when he'll return. It could be days, it could be weeks, and it could be months."

"It could be minutes," she retorted. "Because a bride doesn't know the hour of her bridegroom's return, she must be ready at all times. He may come in the night when you least expect it. Will you be prepared? Or will you weep because you weren't ready?"

We walked Tova to the springs, which were

full with recent rainwater. Mother and I reclined on the grassy banks while Tova submerged herself several times and rubbed herself clean and raw. We returned to the tent, where Mother pulled out bowls and pouches and brushes. I had no idea she knew so much about cosmetics and beauty treatments. She surprised Tova and me. I know the time will come when I'll be subjected to these rituals as well, but I'm glad it isn't now.

Tova's face scrunched up in comic fashion when Mother made her chew on herbs to sweeten her breath. Then, to top it off, Mother mixed up porridge and incense and rolled the mixture into little balls. She forced Tova to squeeze them between her limbs and her body. This was to repel body odor! As if Tova had body odor to begin with! I laughed so hard, it sent Tova and Mother into fits of giggles as well.

A smidgen of olive oil was worked into her hair, and then her locks were brushed until they hung over her shoulders like a black silk curtain. A few more drops of oil were rubbed on her elbows, her knees, and her feet. Her lips and cheeks were painted with red ochre mixed with fat to give them a ripe, healthy appearance.

"This has to be done every day?" Tova asked wearily

"Every day until Guni returns for you."

Mother encourages her to keep a clay lamp filled with oil and a trimmed wick beside her bed. She also has her belongings laid out, ready to be grabbed at a moment's notice.

Now it's just a matter of time.

Two Days Later

Dear diary, the time has come so soon. My sister is gone. Last night, a shout awakened all of us. Tova, conditioned to be prepared at a moment's notice, shot up at once. She wore her day tunic to bed, at mother's urging, so she was already dressed. She lit her lamp, and we raced outside. The night was dark and quiet. Mother and Father each held a burning lamp.

"What happened?" I cried. "Who shouted so?"

"Listen close, Alisah," Father told me, "and you'll know." There was a faint smile on his face.

I heard the rhythmic chirp of the crickets, then the far away hoot of the desert owl. I heard Father's steady breathing on one side of me and Tova's rapid breath on the other.

"Please, Father," I implored him. "What is it? What am I listening for?"

Then I heard it. A clear, steady voice. "Behold the bridegroom cometh! Go ye out to meet him!"

Tova dashed inside the tent, frantic. My eyes were glued to the horizon. One trembling dot of light moved closer and closer until it split into four distinct flames. Three men and Guni rode toward our camp on donkeys. They carried torches in their right hands. At regular intervals, the messenger in the front cried, "Behold the bridegroom cometh! Go ye out to meet him!"

I felt Tova's arms around me. She kissed my face several times, and I reached out and grabbed hold of her hand.

"Tova," I whispered urgently, "before you leave, please tell me one thing. Do you believe you're walking down the path God has chosen for you? If you tell me yes, I'll let you leave with peace in my heart."

My sister held my face in her hands. I'd never seen her look so beautiful. She glowed from within.

"Oh, yes, Alisah. This is the path the Lord has chosen for me, and I'm filled with sudden joy. Now, before I leave, please tell me one thing. Do you believe your journey to Isaac's household is the path God has chosen for you? If you tell me yes, I'll be able to leave you with peace in my heart."

We both began to cry. "Oh, yes, Tova. This is most definitely the path that God has chosen for me. I too am filled with sudden joy. Now go to your groom. He's waiting for you."

She pressed herself into Mother and Father's embrace, and Father broke away and reached into the tent. He pulled out a beautiful leather pouch and loosened the string so Tova could peer inside. "Oh!" she cried. I watched her mouth form words, but her voice was lost. Her face was ashen.

"So I'm not as poor as you think, eh, Tova? Now don't disappoint me and faint in front of your groom," he teased her. "This is your *shiluhim*, your dowry. Take it into your future with your fine young man."

I peeked over Tova's shoulder into the bag. There were gold coins. More gold coins than I'd ever seen. "The same waits for you, Alisah, when it's your time to wed," he told me.

The men had reached the outskirts of camp, and Father nudged Tova toward her groom. She looked at us one last time, then lowered her veil to cover her face. Guni met her halfway. He took the bundles from her arms and helped her climb onto her donkey. Her lamp was still in her hand. I reached for Mother's hand and put my arm around Father's waist. He pulled me close. He smelled just like I remembered. Earthy and musky and comforting. He's a man of surprises, my father. He'd set aside money all these years so he could give us proper dowries.

"What now, Father?" I asked. "What happens next?"

"Now Tova and Guni will go to the wedding chamber," he replied. "In time, they'll choose where they will live. Here or there. It's their choice."

I thought of Rebekah following Eliezer on a camel. Her family watched her leave just as we watched Tova. Did they strain their eyes until she faded into a tiny dot in the desert? Did their tears fall like raindrops like ours did? I thought so.

It took such courage and faith for Tova and Rebekah to leave their families for a life they knew nothing about. Rebekah had never even met Isaac. She let the Lord guide her, and by her own admission, she'd been richly blessed.

"Behold the bridegroom cometh! Go ye out to meet him!" Those words continue to reverberate within me and stir my soul. I'm ready to follow the Lord's leading. Wherever he takes me, I'll go, because I've learned that I don't have to lead. I just have to follow him.

At that moment, Father began to whistle again. It was very soft at first and then deeper and more penetrating, until his very soul was set free and he was at peace again. I watched as the burning flames of the procession dissolved into one resplendent star.

Epilogue

The dangerous ground Deborah spoke of to Alisah proved to be prophetic. Fifty-seven years after Esau sold his birthright to Jacob, the trouble between the two brothers, which had bubbled for more than half a century, finally boiled over.

Isaac was 137 years old when a raven flew over the camp. Not long after, he lost his sight. Fearing that death was at hand, he called for Esau. He wanted to bless his firstborn son. Isaac asked Esau to go into the open country and hunt his favorite food. He promised to bestow the blessing when Esau returned.

Rebekah heard the conversation and devised a cunning plan in Esau's absence. She dressed Jacob in Esau's clothes and covered his smooth hands and neck with hairy goatskins. She prepared the tasty food Isaac wanted, and Jacob presented himself to his father, disguised as his brother. Isaac was fooled, and he blessed the wrong son:

> *"Ah, the smell of my son*
>   *is like the smell of a field*
>   *that the* LORD *has blessed.*
> *May God give you of heaven's dew*
>   *and of earth's richness—*
>   *an abundance of grain and new wine.*
> *May nations serve you*
>   *and peoples bow down to you.*
> *Be lord over your brothers,*
>   *and may the sons of your mother bow*
>   *down to you.*
> *May those who curse you be cursed*
>   *and those who bless you be blessed."*
>   *Genesis 27:27–29*

Esau learned of the trickery when he returned, and he begged his father to bless him anyway. Isaac, having already made Jacob lord over Esau, blessed him in a different way:

> *"Your dwelling will be*
>   *away from the earth's richness,*

> *away from the dew of heaven above.*
> *You will live by the sword*
> *and you will serve your brother.*
> *But when you grow restless,*
> *you will throw his yoke*
> *from off your neck."*
>
> *Genesis 27:39–40*

Esau vowed to kill his twin. Rebekah, fearing for Jacob's life, sent her youngest son away. It was to be the last time she would see the son of her heart. She died before he returned.

God honored Isaac's blessing. He promised to bless Jacob and his offspring, and he changed his name to Israel, which means "prince of God." Jacob's marriage to Leah and Rachel, and his union with their maidservants, resulted in the birth of a dozen sons and one daughter. It was through Jacob's twelve sons that the twelve tribes of Israel were formed.

Esau's descendants, called Edomites, became enemies of Israel for centuries to come. Jacob's relationship with his brother was mended after many years. They buried their father together with peace in their hearts. Isaac was 180 years old when he died. He was laid to rest in the cave of Machpelah beside his wife, Rebekah, and his mother and father.

Jacob lived for 147 years and was also buried in the cave of Machpelah. No mention is made of Esau's death, though it is known that he was not buried with his twin or his ancestors.

Deborah lived to a very old age. When she died, Jacob and all who knew her mourned her passing. She was buried beneath an oak tree near Bethel. The ground above her was sodden with tears. It came to be called Allon Bacuth, the "oak of weeping."

Tova returned to her father's household with her new husband and raised five children. With Guni's skills as a shepherd and Father's shrewdness with money, the wealth of the household grew considerably. Mother enjoyed wheat every day for the rest of her long life.

Mary grew up to become one of the most prolific writers of her time, an unheard feat for a woman of her day. She penned numerous scrolls of stories and poetry, many of which found their way into the library of Alexandria. She was forced to write under the assumed name of Marcus Gabinius. No one ever discovered that the acclaimed writer was a woman.

Alisah married her best friend, Crispus, on her fourteenth birthday. They continued to live in Isaac's household for many years. Crispus worked the land and went on the occasional hunt. Alisah bore three children, and she taught all of them how to write.

Shortly after Rebekah's death, Deborah brought Alisah a small package wrapped in linen. She pressed it into her hands and told her that Rebekah desired her to have it. Alisah lifted away the cloth. A gold bracelet, one that had adorned Rebekah's wrist for many years, gleamed against the white fabric.

A small scrap of papyrus was scratched with these simple words: "Remember me always with this love gift—Rebekah."

Lovely Rebekah

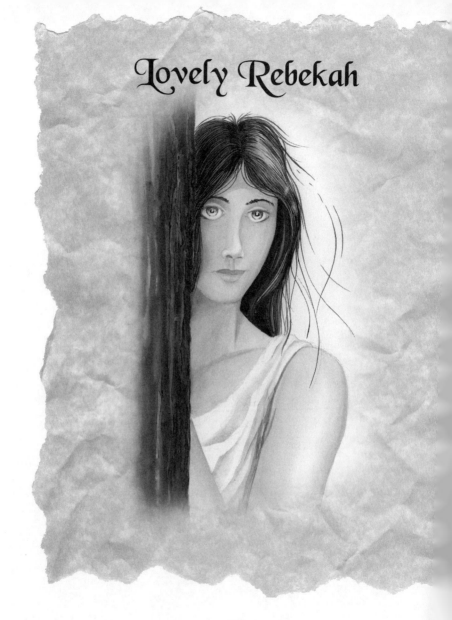

Bundles of unspun fiber, like wool or cotton, were attached to a distaff like this one. Hebrew women, called spinners, wound and twisted the fiber from a distaff to a spindle to make thread.

Isaac and his sons grew all of the food, including wheat and barley, for their household.

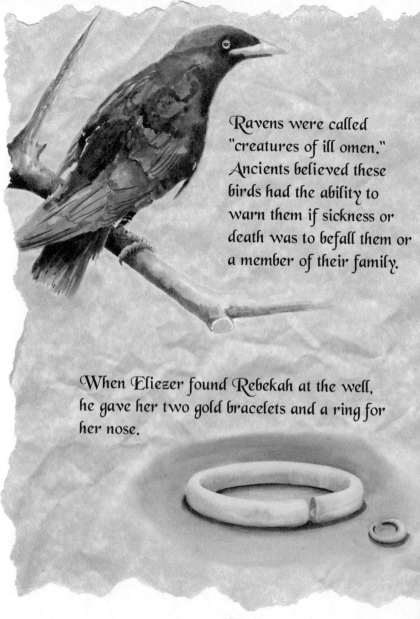

Ravens were called
"creatures of ill omen."
Ancients believed these
birds had the ability to
warn them if sickness or
death was to befall them or
a member of their family.

When Eliezer found Rebekah at the well,
he gave her two gold bracelets and a ring for
her nose.

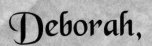

Deborah,

Rebekah's beloved nursemaid.

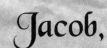

Jacob,

the younger twin, was the favorite of his mother, Rebekah.

Papyrus paper was made from the tall, thick stalks of the papyrus plant, which grew along Egypt's Nile River.

A wooden palette, like this one, was used mostly by scribes. The circular hollows held inkpots, and the reed pens were stored in the area below.

Pots like these were made of clay mixed with sand or crushed stone. They were fired in an oven and then used to serve food, milk, or water.

The Ancient Near East in the Time of Rebekah

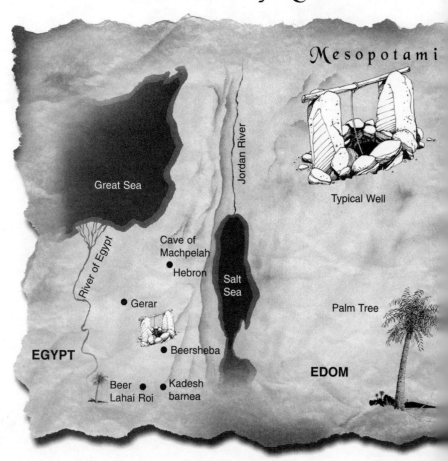

Mesopotami

Typical Well

Great Sea

Jordan River

Cave of Machpelah

● Hebron

Salt Sea

● Gerar

River of Egypt

Palm Tree

● Beersheba

EGYPT

Beer Lahai Roi ● ● Kadesh barnea

EDOM

Alisah's Home

The story begins in Beersheba, on the northern tip of the Negev Desert in Canaan. It moves to Beer Lahai Roi, an oasis about forty miles southwest. It is set (approximately) in the years 1986 B.C. to 1985 B.C.

The People Alisah Wrote of Most

Rebekah: Isaac's wife and mother to Jacob and Esau

Deborah: Rebekah's beloved nursemaid

Herself: Nursemaid in training in Isaac's household*

Tova: Alisah's older sister*

Jacob: Rebekah and Isaac's youngest son and Esau's twin

Esau: Rebekah and Isaac's oldest son and Jacob's twin

The People Alisah Encountered

(In Order of Appearance)

Father: Alisah's father*

Mother: Alisah's mother*

Eliezer: Abraham's most trusted servant

Isaac: Abraham and Sarah's son

Ishmael: Abraham and Hagar's son

Guni: Alisah's suitor*

Zaccai: Guni's father*

Crispus: Young man in Isaac's household and Alisah's friend*

Mary: Girl in Isaac's household *

Claudia: Little girl in Isaac's household*

Julia: Little girl in Isaac's household*

Eunice: Little girl in Isaac's household*

*denotes fictional characters

Tracing History: A Timeline

2026 B.C

Abraham is distressed that his son Isaac is still unmarried. He sends his trusted servant, Eliezer, to find a wife for him in Mesopotamia, the country of Abraham's birth.

The Lord leads Eliezer to Rebekah, and she returns with him. Deborah, her nursemaid, accompanies her. Isaac and Rebekah are married in the tent of his mother, Sarah. He is forty years old.

2006 B.C

After twenty years of marriage, Rebekah gives birth to twins, Esau and Jacob.

1991 B.C

Abraham dies at the age of 175. Isaac and Ishmael, separated for years, put aside their differences to bury their father. He is laid to rest alongside his wife Sarah in the cave of Machpelah.

1985 B.C

Esau sells his birthright to Jacob for a bowl of lentil stew. He later regrets his actions.

1966 B.C

Esau and Jacob are forty years old. Esau marries two pagan women, much to the dismay of Isaac and Rebekah.

1929 B.C

Isaac is 137 years old and blind. He is divinely inspired to pray a blessing over his elder son, Esau. Rebekah tricks her husband, and Isaac unwittingly blesses Jacob instead.

Esau tells his father of the injustice that was committed. Isaac agrees to pray another, different blessing over his firstborn son.

Esau, angry that Jacob denied him his birthright and his father's original blessing, plots to kill his younger brother. Rebekah urges Jacob to flee to her family's home in Haran. Sadly, she never sees her favorite son again.

1922 B.C
Jacob marries Leah and then her sister Rachel.

1929–1886 B.C
Deborah dies at a great, old age. She is buried near Bethel below a tree called Allon Bacuth, which means "oak of weeping."

1886 B.C
Isaac dies. He is 180 years old. Esau and Jacob bury him in the cave of Machpelah near Hebron beside his mother, Sarah, and father, Abraham.

Note: The Bible does not mention the death of Rebekah. It is unknown where in the timeline her death occurred. Genesis 49:31 does tell us that she was buried in the family burial cave in the field of Machpelah.

*Approximate date

Mesopotamia's Place in History

Long ago the vast region between the Tigris and Euphrates rivers in modern day Iraq was called Mesopotamia, which means "the land between the rivers." It is often referred to as the "cradle of civilization," because Sumer, the world's first civilization, was born in the south of Mesopotamia where the two rivers converged.

The Bible contains many references to Mesopotamia, though it is often called by Hebrew names such as Aram, Aram Naharaim, or Paddan Aram. Sometimes the region is referred to by the names of the cities that sprang up within its boundaries or simply by the names of the people who lived there.

Abraham's early home was in Ur of the Chaldees, a city in southern Mesopotamia. He moved from there to Haran, farther north, where he lived until he began his journey to the land of Canaan. Years later Abraham sent Eliezer back to Mesopotamia to pick out a wife for his son Isaac. He told him:

I want you to swear by the LORD, the God of heaven and the God of earth, that you will not get a wife for my son from the daughters of the Canaanites, among whom I am living, but will go to my country and my own relatives and get a wife for my son Isaac.

Genesis 24:3–4

Years later, Jacob also returned to the land of his forefathers when Isaac commanded him:

Do not marry a Canaanite woman. Go at once to Paddan Aram, to the house of your mother's father Bethuel. Take a wife for yourself there, from among the daughters of Laban, your mother's brother.

Genesis 28:1–2

Jacob married both Leah and Rachel, daughters of Laban, and lived in Mesopotamia for many years.

The earliest settlers to this area, the Sumerians, took advantage of the two rivers by building levees and irrigation canals. As a result, they were able to grow barley, wheat, sesame, flax, and a variety of vegetables and fruit. Their villages evolved into self-governing city-states.

Each city-state had its own god or goddess. Tall temples in the shape of stepped pyramids, called ziggurats, were built for them in the center of the villages. The remains of the most famous of these temples lies fifty-six miles south of modern Baghdad. These ruins were once the heart of ancient Babylon in central Mesopotamia, the city founded by Nimrod, the great-grandson of Noah.

Excavations at the site uncovered the remains of a ziggurat thought to have been seven stories tall. It is believed to be part of the famous Tower of Babel mentioned in the Book of Genesis.

An inscription by Nebuchadnezzar II was found on the temple tower. It read in part, "I have completed its magnificence with silver, gold. . . . Since a remote time, people had abandoned it, without order expressing their words."

One of the king's greatest achievements was the hanging gardens of Babylon, one of the seven wonders of the ancient world. The structure has been compared to an artificial mountain, four hundred square feet in diameter and at least eighty feet high, with raised terraces filled with trees and plants. The gardens were watered by a chain pump, which lowered buckets into the Euphrates River and delivered the water to the top.

Nebuchadnezzar is also remembered as the king who captured Judah and laid siege to Jerusalem. Daniel and thousands of Israelites were taken to Babylon, where they were held captive for more than seventy years.

Ancient Mesopotamia made a number of valuable contributions that have affected the modern era. One was the use of cuneiform, a system of writing developed in about 3000 B.C. A pointed stylus was used to make wedge-shaped pictures and marks on wet clay tablets. The tablets were first dried in the sun and later fired in kilns to make the writing permanent.

Once dry, they could be stored or transported.

This system of writing was first invented to keep careful record of business transactions, but it had another purpose. In early cultures writing was believed to possess magical properties. If one could write his or her neighbor's name, he or she was believed to possess power over that person. Cuneiform was used in Mesopotamia and many other Near Eastern cultures for more two thousand years.

Other important inventions of the Mesopotamians include the water clock, the twelve-month calendar based on lunar cycles, the wheel, the early chariot, the plow, and the sailboat.

Then and Now

Beersheba was the northern gateway to the Negev Desert. It was located sixty miles north of the river of Egypt (the Nile) and nearly midway between the southern end of the Salt Sea (the Dead Sea) and the Great Sea (the Mediterranean). It was a welcome oasis in the dry, desolate wilderness that surrounded it. This area received little annual rainfall, but Beersheba's water supply came from underground streams tapped into by a cluster of wells.

The name Beersheba, which means "well of the oath," was first given to a well dug by Abraham. It was by this well that Abraham and Abimelech, king of Gerar, made a peace treaty that allowed them and their future offspring to live together peacefully. Later it became home to Isaac and Jacob.

Modern Beersheba, or Beer Sheva, is slightly southwest of the old town. There is an archaeological dig just outside of the city called Tel Sheva, which is the site of Beersheba during the reign of King Solomon. Arabs still call it Bir es-Seba, meaning "well of the seven," because of the two large wells and five smaller ones that have survived since ancient times.

Today the population of Beersheba includes local Bedouins (nomadic Arabs), Israelis, Ethiopians, and Russians. The city has a thriving cultural center with many museums, a symphony, and historical monuments that pay tribute to its long and interesting history. Beersheba is also home to Israel's famous Ben Gurion University.

The Negev was a desert region south of Judea that covered an area of about five thousand square miles. It was triangular in shape, with its base just above Beersheba and its apex at Elath.

There were four separate regions: a coastal plain in the northwest, a plateau in the center, mountains in the south, and a valley in the east. Often referred to as "the wilderness," the Negev received less than ten inches of rain per year, and much of the land was dry and sparse with little vegetation. Oases, like Beersheba and Beer Lahai Roi, were scattered between long stretches of barren wasteland.

Nabatean nomads who roamed the Negev not only survived, but prospered in the desert wilderness. They took advantage of the rainy season by collecting the water in cisterns. Some of them even built reservoirs and dams.

They grew quite wealthy in the spice trade by leading the spice caravans from Arabia and Somalia north through the desert. When the Negev was incorporated into the Roman Empire, the Nabateans raise thoroughbred horses, which were raced in the Roman coliseums.

The Bedouins, also desert dwellers, were a common sight in the Negev. Like the biblical nomads Abraham and Isaac, they moved frequently with their sheep, goats, donkeys, and camels in tow. They followed the water sources and lived off the land. Their black tents, made of woven goats' hair, were resistant to the rain, wind, and sun.

Today the Bedouins can still be found in the

Negev, often settled near towns like Beer Sheva. Here they bring their handiwork such as woven rugs, cushions, camel saddles, and Arab head-dresses to sell on market day. Buyers and sellers conduct their business in silence, using long stares and occasional blinks and smiles to negotiate a price or wrap up a sale.

Bibliography

Many sources were consulted and used in research for writing Alisah's and Rebekah's story in The Promised Land Diaries series, including:

Adam Clarke's Commentary on the Bible, Adam Clarke, abridged by Ralph H. Earle (World Bible Publishing Co., 1996).

Atlas of the Bible: An Illustrated Guide to the Holy Land, edited by Joseph L. Gardner (The Readers Digest Association, 1981).

The Biblical Times, edited by Derek Williams (Baker Book House Company, 1997).

Jamieson, Fausset, and Brown's Commentary on the Whole Bible, *Fausset*, Brown, Robert Jamieson (Zondervan, 1999).

Matthew Henry's Commentary on the Whole Bible: Complete and Unabridged in One Volume, Matthew Henry (Hendrickson Publishers, 1991).

Meredith's Book of Bible Lists, J. L. Meredith (Bethany House Publishers, 1980).

Nelson's Illustrated Encyclopedia of the Bible, edited by John Drane (Thomas Nelson, Inc., 2001).

The New International Dictionary of the Bible, revising editor J. D. Douglas, general editor Merrill C. Tenney (Zondervan, 1987).

The Picture Bible Dictionary, Berkeley and Alvera Mickelsen (Chariot Books, an imprint of David C. Cook Publishing Co., 1993).

Women of the Bible: A One-Year Devotional Study of Women in Scripture, Ann Spangler and Jean Syswerda (Zondervan Publishing House, 1999).

About the Author

Anne Tyra Adams is the author of eight children's books, several of which have been translated into three foreign languages: Indonesian, Korean, and Afrikaans. Two of her books, *The New Kids Book of Bible Facts* and *The Baker Book of Bible Travels for Kids,* provided the foundation for writing this series, the Promised Land Diaries.

A journalist and detailed researcher, Adams is also a "student of ancient history," with a deep fascination for the Jewish culture. She used all this experience, love of history, and curiosity to write this book.

When not working on more Promised Land Diaries, Adams loves to read the classics and ancient history, taking many armchair travels in time to foreign lands. She especially loves reading biographies of famous authors.

She and her husband and their two children live in Phoenix, Arizona. They often hike in the mountainous desert surrounding their home and have been known to spot quail, coyote, an occasional fox, and many lizards. Not to be outdone by the great outdoors, they share their home with three dogs, a cat, and an assortment of little fish.

About the Illustrator

Dennis Edwards is the illustrator of three big Bible story-books: *Heroes of the Bible, Boys Life Adventures,* and *My Bible Journey.* As a designer and illustrator he's also contributed to numerous others.

His favorite books include Robert Louis Stevenson's *Treasure Island,* comic books, and science fiction-related books because "the sky's the limit!"

Dennis also enjoys acting, and at times gets to perform for the kids at his church.

Books in

Series

1
Persia's Brightest Star
The Diary of Queen Esther's Attendant

2
The Laughing Princess of the Desert
The Diary of Sarah's Traveling Companion

3
Priceless Jewel at the Well
The Diary of Rebekah's Nursemaid

4
The Peaceful Warrior
The Diary of Deborah's Armor Bearer

The author would like to thank Jerry Watkins, Todd
Watkins, the staff of Educational Publishing Concepts,
Jeanette Thomason for her excellent editorial guidance, and
the rest of the team of Baker Book House Company, as well
as the talented Dennis Edwards and Donna Diamond.

Dedicated with love to my children Michal Tyra and
Alexandra Tyra.

© 2004 by Baker Book House Company

Published by Baker Books
a division of Baker Book House Company
P.O. Box 6287, Grand Rapids, MI 49516-6287
www.bakerbooks.com

Printed in the United States of America

Library of Congress Cataloging-in-Publication Data is on file at the Library of Congress,
Washington, D.C.

ISBN 0-8010-4526-6

Scripture is taken from the HOLY BIBLE, NEW INTERNATIONAL VERSION®. NIV®. Copyright ©
1973, 1978, 1984 by International Bible Society. Used by permission of Zondervan. All rights reserved.

Series Creator: Jerry Watkins and Educational Publishing Concepts, with Anne Tyra Adams
Cover Illustrator: Donna Diamond
Designer and Illustrator: Dennis Edwards
Editors: Jeanette Thomason, Kelley Meyne

The biblical account of Rebekah can be found in the Bible's Old Testament/Book of Genesis, chapters
24–28. While Alisah's diaries and the epilogue are based on this and historical accounts, the character of
Alisah, her diaries, and some of the minor events described are works of fiction.